SPEAK ILL OF THE DEAD

SPEAK ILL
OF THE DEAD

Peter Chambers

CHIVERS
THORNDIKE

This Large Print book is published by BBC Audiobooks Ltd, Bath, England and by Thorndike Press®, Waterville, Maine, USA.

Published in 2005 in the U.K. by arrangement with the author.
Published in 2005 in the U.S. by arrangement with Peter Chambers.

U.K. Hardcover ISBN 1–4056–3150–3 (Chivers Large Print)
U.K. Softcover ISBN 1–4056–3151–1 (Camden Large Print)
U.S. Softcover ISBN 0–7862–7011–X (Nightingale)

The text of this Large Print edition is unabridged.
Other aspects of the book may vary from the original edition.

Set in 16 pt. New Times Roman.

Printed in Great Britain on acid-free paper.

British Library Cataloguing in Publication Data available

Library of Congress Cataloging-in-Publication Data

Chambers, Peter, 1924–
    Speak ill of the dead / Peter Chambers.
       p.   cm.
    ISBN 0–7862–7011–X (lg. print : sc : alk. paper)
    1. Large type books. I. Title.
PR6066.H463S68 2004
823'.914   2004057984

CHAPTER ONE

She was a faded little woman, and she sat nervously clasping and unclasping the brass clip on her purse. Her age could have been anywhere between thirty-five and fifty, and she wasn't doing a great deal by way of her appearance to indicate that it mattered how old she was. The name was Carter, Mrs. Erasmus Carter Junior, and it was evident from the birdie glances she darted all around the room that Mrs. Erasmus Carter Junior was not in the habit of calling on private investigators or persons of that type.

I smiled at her encouragingly, as I thought. Her reaction was an expression of near panic. It would have come as no surprise if she'd leaped from the chair, and jumped out the window. Looking back on it, I almost wish she had.

'Well now Mrs. Carter, just what can I do to help you?'

She cleared her throat, a quick barking sound.

'Mr. Preston, maybe I'm doing the wrong thing in coming here.'

'That is hard for me to judge without knowing something about it,' I encouraged.

The day was hot, and I had no wish to listen to Mrs. Carter's little troubles, whatever they might be. I had a wish to be out at Palmtrees Racetrack, where some very promising nags were lined up. Trouble was, I'd been misled quite a bit recently by promising nags who failed to live up to their promise, so you could say I needed the work.

My prospective client gave the purse some more action before taking me into her confidence.

'Do you help find people?' she queried.

'Sometimes, yes. Is that the kind of enquiry you have in mind?'

The mouse-haired head wagged up and down so vigorously I feared for her spinal cord.

'Yes. My sister, Anthea.'

Then she clammed up again. Sighing inwardly, I spread out a nice clean sheet of paper and unclipped my pen. There are certain types of client who like that. It conveys an impression of order and system which they seem to find reassuring. If they witnessed some of the later disorder they'd be less comforted.

'Perhaps I should take a few details,' I suggested. 'May I have your own given name please?'

She simpered slightly.

'Why yes, it's Cornelia.'

Cornelia and Anthea. Somebody had to be kidding. 'And your address Mrs. Carter?'

'Well, I don't have an address. That is to

say—well—I guess you'd best have my aunt's. You see, she's very unwell, and she doesn't have anyone too look after her. As I've only just arrived back, it seems natural I should do it.'

Again I smiled, to show I understood.

'And where exactly would that be?'

'Orange Patch, Little Falls, near Fresno.'

I wrote that down carefully.

'You say you're looking after your aunt? Is it a farm?'

'Oh, yes. A fruit farm. But I don't interfere with that, naturally. There's a foreman who sees to all that side of things. It's just as well,' and she fluttered a hand, 'I'm afraid I wouldn't be very much help.'

That I can believe, I thought inwardly.

'I take it you haven't been there very long?'

Any extraction of useful information promised to be a slow business. She shook her head.

'No. About a month. You see I've been overseas for many years. In Africa. Mr. Carter had an important position there you know.'

She paused to be certain I had taken the point.

'Really? And now he's been brought home?'

To my dismay, she gave a sudden wail and dived into the purse. Producing a pink lace square which smelled violently of toilet water she dabbed madly at her eyes.

'Oh no,' she moaned. 'I couldn't bring him

home. He's buried out there, in that infernal place, among all those terrible people. Poor dear Erasmus. And he did so want to die here at home.'

A few more wails, then she gradually subsided. A few final sniffs, and a further flurry of the useless pink handkerchief.

'I'm sorry, I hadn't meant to—er—'

'Please,' I begged, 'I quite understand. So you had to come back to the States, and for the moment you're staying with your aunt. Now, tell me about Anthea.'

She looked wistful then.

'It all seems so silly now, looking back. We quarrelled, you know.'

I was gradually learning that every other sentence ended with that supposition. It wasn't that my visitor really expected me to know at all. Merely a figure of speech.

'What was the quarrel about?' I prompted.

'Oh it all seemed terribly important at the time. If only young people could realize that these quarrels are easily started, often very painful and difficult to end. And yet, when they get older they know in their hearts that there is only really the family that counts. The trouble is, by that time it's sometimes too late to do anything about it.'

'That is very true,' I said gravely.

It was also very true that Mrs. Carter had been away from her family for years, and but for the death of the unfortunate Erasmus, she would still be in Africa. She might have been thinking about her sister, but I doubted very much whether she would have been doing anything else about it.

'But then,' she went on, 'we were young. Anthea was always a hot-tempered—no, I shouldn't say that, she was always very impulsive. Yes, that's it, impulsive. I had only known Mr. Carter for a short while, and then she had this crazy idea that she was going to become an actress. Well, you can imagine the family reaction to that.'

How was I supposed to imagine any such thing, when I knew nothing of the family, was not clear. I did my nodding act again.

'I mean she had a good position as a stenographer, with the largest sales organization in town. If that dreadful man hadn't put such ridiculous thoughts into her head, I'm certain everything would have been all right.'

'Ah, there was a man involved. Are you able to tell me anything about him?'

The pale lips wrinkled in distaste.

'I certainly am. His name was Walstrom—so he said—'

'Could you spell that please?'

She spelled it out slowly and I looked at the end product.

'Sounds Scandinavian, Swedish perhaps or Danish?'

'I've no idea,' she sniffed. 'His other name

was Joseph, I remember that.'

'And I gather this Walstrom began persuading your sister that she ought to go into the theater?'

'Theater?' she scoffed. 'Oh no, by no means. If that had been the case, the reaction might have been different. After all, in these modern times, some quite *decent* people got into the theater. Why one of our own neighbor's daughters did that, and she's becoming quite famous in a modest way.'

'Then, what exactly did Walstrom have in mind?'

'Oh he said she ought to start by becoming a model. Now, I don't know what that means here in Monkton City, Mr. Preston, but I can assure you we know exactly what it means back home.'

Well, back home wasn't so different from Monkton in some ways at least.

'Mrs. Carter, I know what you mean naturally. However, I ought to point out that modelling is a prominent and profitable section of the entertainment world.'

'I realize that,' she replied. 'But how many people who call themselves models have ever really done any respectable professional work?'

Mrs. Carter was by no means entirely alfalfa. I smiled.

'As to the proportion, I haven't any idea at all. This man you mentioned, Walstrom, what

6

was his occupation?'

'That was another thing. None of us really knew, including Anthea herself. He said he was a promoter, but he was terribly vague about details. The man was such an obvious slicker—'

I tried not to grin as the word came out.

'—anybody but my young sister could see through him at a glance.'

'What was he doing in your home town? And where was that, incidentally?'

'South Creek, Idaho. It's less than an hour by road from Pocatello itself.'

She implied by her tone that I needn't imagine she was a stranger to the ways of the big city. With Pocatello, Idaho, less than an hour away by road. I looked impressed as I wrote it down.

'Now you were asking me, oh yes, what Joe Walstrom was doing there. I certainly haven't the remotest idea, but this much I know. Whatever he was doing, it didn't seem to include any work. He was always to be found if needed. Usually at Sharkey's Pool Room or in some bar. If he was working, I don't believe anyone ever caught him in the act, you know?'

'What did he look like, this man?'

She knitted up her face in concentration.

'Now, let me see. He wasn't what you'd call tall, not really tall. Probably about five feet nine inches. Very black hair, smothered in some revolting cream, parted in the center. He was quite a good-looking man, I will say that. You've seen pictures of those old-time movie stars with those dear little toothbrush moustaches? Joe Walstrom could easily have passed for one of those.'

'You mean, the latin lover kind of face?'

She blushed slightly and lowered her eyes.

'Why yes, I guess that is exactly what I'm trying to say.'

'Clothes?'

'Dreadful. Really quite dreadful. I mean, I like a man to be neat. But this man was no more than a—a—'

'Clothes horse?' I suggested.

I'd got the wrong woman. She looked at me blankly. 'What I mean is, a tailor's dummy,' I corrected. Her face cleared, and she nodded.

'That's it precisely. A tailor's dummy. Always everything too perfect, and he wore jewelery too. Two or three rings on his hands, a watch encrusted with what he claimed were diamonds. That kind of thing, you know?'

I knew the kind of thing. From the sound of him, Mr. Walstrom wouldn't be too hard to track down. Always providing he was anywhere near Monkton City, that is.

'Fine, that's a most helpful description,' I encouraged.

I meant it, too. Most of the descriptions I get couldn't be relied on to identify one white man amid a tribe of Zulu.

'So your sister left town with Walstrom and

8

came here?'

'Yes. Mind you, it was fourteen years ago, and the only word we've had in all that time was a handful of postcards the first few weeks. Since then, nothing.'

Fourteen years, I reflected hopelessly. It was a lifetime. The sister could be anywhere by now. But I tried not to show what I was thinking.

'It's a long time ago,' I said slowly. 'Did Anthea include any return address on those cards?'

'Yes. Nine Two Five, Pioneer Street. You know where that is?'

I did. I also knew enough about Pioneer Street to give my new client the heeby jeebies. But that is no part of the service.

'I know it well. Now, if I could just have a description of your sister. I know it will be out of date, but we never know what will be useful.'

'I can do better,' she said triumphantly. 'I just knew you were going to ask me that, and I've brought along a picture.'

Better and better. I took the creased snapshot from her, and took a look at Anthea. It was a full-length picture of a young girl, nineteen or twenty years old. She had a froth of bright blonde hair, and the face was heavily made up. Too heavily for the daylight, with the result that the features were slightly blurred.

'This is the best one you have?'

'Yes it is. And of course, she won't look like that today.'

This was offered with a quiet vindictiveness, which was not at all attractive to the ear. I laid the picture on the desk.

'One last thing, Mrs. Carter. The family name.'

'Horan. We were the Horan girls. That is my aunt's name also, the one I'm staying with at the moment.'

'Speaking of your aunt, is there a telephone at the farm?'

She told me the number, and I wrote that down too. Now I had all the relevant information I was likely to get, and I could usher my client out. But she was not quite finished. She rested one gloved hand on the desk and looked at me hopefully.

'Mr. Preston, I'm thankful to say I am not a poor woman. I'm quite prepared to spend a fair sum of money to locate Anthea once more.'

I didn't have to pretend to look cheerful this time.

'There's no denying these things can be expensive,' I admitted. 'I may find I have to help people's memories along with the odd few dollars. Which of course will be accounted to you.'

'Good. But I don't think you should spend too long on this. I imagine you will know within a day or two whether or not you are

10

likely to be successful?'

'A day or two isn't very long,' I hedged. 'Surprising how many different leads one can get, and ninety per cent of them useless.'

'I understand that. But I would ask you to be in touch by Friday. Tell me how far you've got, and we can then decide whether it is worthwhile for you to continue.'

Mrs. Carter was laying it on the line. I needn't think, she was telling me, that this case was destined to carry me into a comfortable old age.

'I'll call you Friday,' I promised. 'And now, if there's nothing else you have to tell me—'

She rose and extended a limp hand which I shook.

'Till Friday then. And I needn't tell you how I'll be praying for your success.'

She went out in a cloud of talcum and rosewater, a dried sort of woman, unattractive and pushing middle age hard. In a way, I hoped I'd find Anthea Horan, for her sister's sake. She wasn't the kind who would make friends too readily, and a sister in the background would help alleviate the loneliness she was almost certainly facing.

Looking down at the notes I'd made, I didn't feel too optimistic. Small town gal lured to big city by smoothie. And fourteen years ago into the bargain. The old movie moguls used to have a saying. Five miles east of Los Angeles there is a cornfield. It stretches clear across the dear old U.S.A. spreading north and south. Five miles short of New York it comes to an end. They didn't want slick or sick or message movies. They wanted plots the farmers could follow, with a few tears thrown in so the farmer's daughter went along too. By the mid-30s they had refined the formula down to five basic scripts. And the story of Anthea Horan was one of the five. It was old as the hills, and even if it had happened fourteen days ago, I might have had trouble in locating the errant sister. But fourteen years? I shrugged, folded the sheet of paper and slipped it in a drawer. If I was to collect two days' pay from Mrs. Carter, the least I could do was pretend to follow up all these hot leads she'd given me. Outside Florence Digby looked up from her typewriter. As usual she looked cool and immaculate in a crisp lime-green cotton suit.

'Mrs. Carter is now a client,' I told her. 'Start booking my time as of now.'

'Very well. And, by the way, Sam Thompson called in to see if you had anything for him to do. He's broke again.'

I shook my head. Thompson works for me whenever he is driven to doing any work at all. He has an incorrigible thirst and a deep disinclination for any form of labor, two things which are famously incompatible. So when the bartenders start making hard remarks about outstanding debts, Sam reports reluctantly for duty. But I hadn't anything for him to do, not right then.

'Sorry,' I regretted. 'There's nothing in this for him. I'll call him if anything turns up.'

It was hot outside. The Chev seemed inclined to turn its nose towards the cool green grass out at Palmtrees, but I pointed the old girl firmly towards the tough end of town.

CHAPTER TWO

I headed for Pioneer Street, which is a side turning off Conquest Street. Conquest is that street in your town, every town, which the city fathers are always about to clean up. It starts off in fine style, with a legitimate theater right on the corner, and half facing the prosperous business district. Then there are a few good restaurants, Chinese, Spanish, Hungarian and so forth. After that the tone lowers gradually. By the time you are three blocks along Conquest, other forms of amusement begin to appear. Jazz cellars, girlie shows, private movies (members only), health clubs. We have a saying in Monkton that the man who can bring some new form of diversion to Conquest is half-way to a quick fortune. But it is an empty saying, because the kind of diversion you can't find somewhere along that infamous mile doesn't exist.

In broad daylight the place is savagely exposed. The dirt and the grime and the cracks are all searched out by the merciless sun. The peeling paint of the shoddy façades, the wires dangling from the neon signs. And everywhere the overriding smell of a thousand dishes being prepared in a hundred greasy spoons. But the daylight has its compensations. You are unlikely to be mugged if you pass too close to a doorway. The hookers are also far more reticent, those few who happen to be up and around at such an unearthly hour as three in the afternoon. The barkers outside the various sparkling attractions have not yet picked up their full steam. The so-called male nurses outside the health clubs and gymnasiums are not so pressing in their attentions. So I was able to proceed unmolested deep into the heart of what one enthusiastic councilman called 'this cancer on the soul of our fair city.'

Turning right into Pioneer Street, I wondered what Anthea Horan from South Creek, Idaho, must have felt when she first saw the place. Nine Two Five turned out to be a bar and grill with some rooms above. There didn't seem to be any outside access to the upper floors so I pushed the wooden swing gates and went inside.

Considering the street, the interior wasn't half-bad. There was a faded carpet on the floor and the tables looked clean. To alleviate the gloom there were a few wall-lights, and

14

even these had shades. The place was called the Four Horsemen, and it seemed apt, to judge by the way the clientele had their noses buried in racing sheets. They didn't look up, but I knew I'd been examined carefully the second I opened the door. At the bar a big bald-headed man watched my approach.

'Beer,' I told him.

He slopped a mug of foaming suds in front of me, made change from the dollar bill I extended.

'I'm looking for somebody,' I confided.

Behind me, papers rustled and I could feel eyes on my back. The bartender stared at me.

'Who isn't?' he shrugged.

'How long has this place been here?'

'What is it, a quiz? Listen, I just serve the drinks. You wanta drink, I serve you. That's all I know.'

I had the feeling he was looking at somebody behind me. Taking out some bills, I put ten on the counter.

'All I want is some simple information. I want to know about things that happened here years ago. Nothing to cause any trouble for anybody now.'

'Years ago?' he repeated hopefully. 'How many years?'

'Fourteen.'

The relief on his face was widespread. He chuckled.

'Fourteen years ago? You have to be

kidding mister.'

'No I don't. A girl left home, gave this address.' I put the print of Anthea in front of him. 'That was how she looked then. Does it mean anything?'

He squinted at it hard, shook his head.

'We don't get that kind of dame in here. This ain't no country club.'

'What seems to be the trouble?'

A new voice came over my shoulder. I turned to find a slim white-faced man looking at me.

'This guy is full of questions, Mister Dee,' complained the barkeep.

Mr. Dee opened his eyes wider.

'Really? Well, I'm the owner here. Come and sit down, maybe I can help.'

I took my beer along to the corner table where he'd been sitting.

'The name is Preston,' I told him. 'I'm looking for a girl who ran away from home years ago.'

'Why here?'

'She gave this address.'

'Ah. I'm afraid you won't get much help here now. I only bought the place two years ago. Anything earlier than that, I wouldn't know.'

'Does anyone live on those floors above here?' I persisted.

'Just myself and my own people. No runaway girls. Girls are girls and business is

16

business. I keep the two things far apart Mr. Preston.'

I nodded. The visit was about as useless as I'd expected.

'I wasn't very hopeful,' I admitted. 'Thanks for your time, Mr. Dee. By the by you wouldn't know a Joe Walstrom? Kind of a handsome guy, a dresser?'

'No. I don't believe I ever heard the name.'

'One last thing. Would you mind telling me the previous owners?'

'Not at all. It was a company called A.B. Amusements. I dealt with a Los Angeles lawyer named Davis, er wait a minute, Elmo Davis.'

'I'm much obliged.'

I finished the beer and went out. The racing papers didn't move. As I was about to step into the Chev, feet pounded behind me.

'Hey you, Mister.'

I waited as a short, tubby man panted to a halt.

'Well?'

'Back—' he gulped air. 'Back there. In the Horseman. I was there.'

'And?'

'Maybe I can help.'

He peered at me through fat greedy eyes.

'How's if we get in the car? Bad for my feet standing on this hot concrete.'

'All right.'

We climbed in, my new companion grunting

17

and puffing as he wedged himself in the seat.

'You're trying to find out something happened a long time ago. That it?'

'Not quite,' I corrected. 'I'm trying to trace someone who went missing a long time ago. Here's a picture of her. Ring any bells?'

He looked at the picture, still breathing puffily as he did so.

'Nice looking gal,' he muttered. 'Course, we used to get a lot of 'em back in those days. You know, when the Four Horsemen was really the Four Horsemen.'

He looked at me to be certain I understood. I didn't.

'I'm not following you,' I admitted. 'What was so different in those days?'

'I'm telling you,' he complained. 'The joint used to jump, then. We had dames like this one coming in by the train load. Upstairs, you know where Dee lives now, that was a big model agency then. Yes,' he leaned back his head, and his eyes sparkled. 'Back them days, a man could see maybe ten or twelve beautiful dames coming in and going out, all for the price of a beer. The joint was hot as a stove.'

I began to get very interested in the fat man. He refused an Old Favorite, but I didn't, drawing heavily on the white tube.

'This sounds interesting,' I confided. 'What is your name?'

'Me? I'm Tuborg, Tubby Tuborg. I don't need to tell you everybody calls me Tubby

18

the Tuba.'

He chortled happily, quite content to be the roly-poly butt of all that scintillating wit.

'My name is Preston, Mr. Tuborg. If anything you have to tell me looks like finding the girl, I'll see you don't get overlooked.'

All the laughter left his face, and a look of cunning replaced it. I preferred the laughter.

'Yes, well now,' he puffed. 'Just how much do you reckon this information is worth?'

'That I can't say without knowing what it is,' I countered.

'True. But if it leads to the girl? That oughta be worth a bit of money to her old daddy, I guess?'

'She doesn't have a daddy. I'm working for her sister, and she has hardly any money at all. Tell you what, I might be able to spread, say, twenty-five.'

His mouth curled downwards.

'Twenty-five bucks? Then we don't have anything to talk about do we? It wasn't worth coming out in the sunshine for that kind of money. I guess I had the wrong number.'

He pressed the door handle, and made to get out. I put a hand on his wrist. Suddenly I was very interested in Tubby.

'Just a minute. Maybe twenty-five is not the key to Fort Knox. But it's fair pay for half an hour of your time. Anybody's time. Why are you turning me down?'

He shrugged, and his shins wobbled to

19

a halt.

'No use stirring up all that old stuff for peanuts. Best leave it lay.'

He was avoiding my eyes, taking care not to see me. Slowly, I shook my head.

'You're a liar, Mr. Tuborg.'

'I don't have to sit here—'

'Shut up. You're a liar. You came out here to find out how the market runs. Now you find it's only twenty-five dollars and you want to duck out. Look at you, Mr. Tuborg. A forty dollar suit, cracked shoes and a worn shirt. You don't need twenty-five bucks the way I don't need twenty-five million. No, you're turning things over in your greedy little mind. If it's worth twenty-five for me to find out something, then it's worth more to somebody else not to have that thing found out. You're thinking of starting an auction, Tubby.'

He sneered uncertainly.

'Yeah? Well, what about it? There ain't any law says I gotta tell you a damned thing. And I ain't gonna. So you can go straight to hell, Mr. Preston.'

I felt anger rise inside me. Here was this fat slob, who could probably tell me something very useful, spitting in my face. I wanted to beat it out of him, but in the same moment I knew it was childish.

'Get out Fatso, while you're still in one piece. I'll come back and see you again, when you've decided whether to play both ends against the middle.'

He must have sensed my mood, because he was out of that seat like a startled jack rabbit, and heading back for the protection of the Four Horsemen. I watched him scuttle inside, then drove along slowly till I came to the first pay phone.

'Preston Investigations,' came Florence Digby's voice.

'Miss Digby, I'm on Pioneer Street in the nine hundreds. Can you contact Thompson please, and have him get over here on the run? You know where he is?'

'For once, Mr. Preston, yes I do. I'll get him right away.'

I climbed back into the car, which was rapidly becoming a sweat-box in the blistering sun. I could see the Four Horsemen in my rear mirror, and I settled down to watch the doorway while I waited for Thompson. Minutes ticked slowly by, once or twice I almost fell asleep. It was nearly half an hour later that the passenger door opened.

'You could've picked a street with some shade in it,' grumbled Thompson.

I kept my eyes on the mirror, and told Sam about the Four Horsemen and Tubby Tuborg. I was very careful as to detail in describing the man. It wouldn't be much help to have Thompson traipsing all over town after the wrong man.

'This could be a long one, Sam. What I'm

hoping is that the fat man will call somebody, may have already done it. With luck, he ought to go and see this somebody to collect whatever they think it's worth to keep his mouth shut.'

'And I get to follow him, see who this other party is,' he finished.

'Right.'

'Er, a question?'

'Go ahead.'

'Just as easy for the other guy to come here,' he suggested. 'The only way I can be sure about that is from inside.'

I'd already thought about the possibility.

'No, I don't think so. Always assuming I'm right at all, this other man won't be anxious to come near the place. If he's willing to pay money to have his connections forgotten, he'd be a fool to re-establish them himself.'

And my second reason, which I didn't voice, was that I didn't want Thompson spending a period of possibly hours inside a bar.

'Yeah,' he agreed grudgingly. 'That makes sense. Car fare? I may need to grab a cab in a hurry.'

I passed over ten.

'It has to be accounted for. This isn't one of my millionaire clients. Just a worried woman with a small income.'

'Okay, okay. How long do you want to run this picture?'

'Till you get something, or the guy goes

to bed.'

He muttered something about chain gangs and sweated labor, and the rights of the individual. I grinned and turfed him out of the car. So long as Thompson is grumbling, I know he's all right. I drove out of the neighborhood and down to our small artistic quarter. It isn't much, just a few studios and the local teevee station, by the way some of the local characters behave, you'd think it was the left bank of the Seine.

I pulled up outside one of the more respectable looking buildings and went in. My man has a studio on the third floor. His name is Daniel Crompton and he is just about the biggest name in the photographic world in town. I'd known him on and off for years, and he ought to be good for some information.

Nobody answered my knock and I opened the door, sliding my head around. In the center of the huge room was a beach chair, lounging variety. Displayed on this was a long-legged blonde, lounging variety. Dan was pulling a hefty arc lamp into place.

'There, that's it. All right honey, you know what I want.'

He stood about four feet from her, bringing a small camera up to his eye.

'Fine, that's fine. Now I want you to start off by looking at that door, then bring your head slowly round towards me and past. Just smile, but keep your mouth closed. We're not advertising gum health. Go.'

The girl moved her head gradually around in an arc. All the time Dan was pressing away at the instantaneous shutter.

'Good. Good. Now roll on to your stomach and repeat the dose. And will you keep that mouth shut, honey. You can show me your teeth afterwards.'

He dropped to one knee and again came the rapid click-click as he exposed frame after frame.

'Well,' he said tiredly, 'I guess that'll have to do. Get the fur coat on will you and we'll knock off that stuff for Harp—'

He stopped talking, realizing she was looking at something else. I was the something else. Dan swivelled round and saw me.

'You picked a fine time for socializing,' he grumbled. 'I have two girls go sick on me today and I'm way behind.'

'Nice to see you too,' I assured him. 'But this won't take a minute Dan, and it's important.'

'I can imagine. Needless to say, it's of no importance at all that millions of readers are waiting with baited breath for the next Crompton masterpiece. Oh, all right. Chloe, take five. And don't put that coat on till I tell you. The people want to see a pretty face, not a melted package of lard.'

She winked at me and went out.

'Nice-looking lard they're packing these

days.'

He looked at me with pain.

'I don't want to hear your adolescent sex yearnings,' he snapped. 'In this racket it's just so much meat on the hoof. And I really am busy, Mark.'

'Right. I want you to remember something. Something in your own line.'

'Try me.'

'I'm working on a lead, and I've come up with a place called the Four Horsemen. Mean anything?'

'Not so far.'

'It seems possible there was some trouble there involving photography. It would be some time back, maybe years. It could have been art pictures in the plain wrapper, blue movies, I don't know. Something of the kind, I imagine.'

He sucked at a forefinger and thought.

'No,' he decided. 'No Four Horsemen. The only good case I can recall of that kind was an art posing dodge, but that was a place called Studio Six. It was where you'd expect, somewhere off Conquest Street.'

I sighed hopefully.

'How about Pioneer Street?'

He clicked his fingers with triumph.

'Yes, that's it. Pioneer Street it was, Studio Six, Pioneer Street.'

'Could be the place,' I said guardedly, 'but I can't be sure. When was all this?'

'Oh, way back. Let's see, oh, six years,

maybe five. Caused a hell of an uproar at the time. Naturally, I was especially interested. Does it help?'

'It does,' I admitted. 'You don't happen to recall any of the people involved?'

He looked at me disdainfully.

'Be your age, Mark. It was big at the time, but I don't have any reason to recall details after all these years. I wasn't involved personally, you know.'

'No, I didn't know, but I'm glad to hear it. Anyway thanks, Dan. I think it may be a real help.'

'Any time. If you find the missing heirlooms do I get a cut in on the reward?'

'Any heirlooms turn up,' I promised solemnly, 'you are in for ten per cent.'

We shook hands quickly and went about our respective affairs. Mine took me to the offices of the *Monkton City Globe*. The day staff would be leaving about this time and the man I wanted was one Shad Steiner, night editor. I knew he'd be there well ahead of his crew, because that's the way Shad is. He was already seated behind his desk in the little glass cubicle he calls an office.

'Ah,' he greeted. 'And what is it you want from me that doesn't have any story value this time?'

'I'm very glad you asked me that, Shad,' I assured him. 'Just by chance I do happen to need a morsel of information.'

'Morsels yet,' he swivelled his eyes. 'A change it'll be from the usual meal you make out of all my red hot news. Well?'

'Some years back, five, six, I'm not really certain, there was some case or other involving a photographic place, Studio Six. It used to be down on Pioneer Street.'

'And?'

'And I'd like your O.K. to have a dig around in the morgue, see what I can find out about it.'

Steiner sighed, looked to heaven for guidance, and placed both hands on the table in front of him.

'So I'll come right out with it. Why?'

'Nothing that would interest you,' I began.

'Don't say that to me,' he snorted. 'Don't tell me what interests me. I'm a newspaper man. Everything interests me. Especially I'm interested in anything important enough for somebody to spend good money hiring an expensive private policeman. So-called. Just tell me what it is doesn't interest me.'

I shrugged off-handedly. As usual I'd have to be careful with Steiner. The guy has a nose for news which is renowned even on the West Coast where that kind of nose is commonplace.

'A missing person deal. Girl quit the farm years ago, headed this way, could have been involved with this Studio Six outfit. I'm supposed to find her.'

27

He stared at me along each side of the great nose.

'Really? I haven't seen that one in thirty years. Let me see, I think it was Lew Ayres and Sally Eilers, but then again I can't be certain. So many people made that picture. What do you think, I'm a shnook?'

I didn't blame him. It certainly sounded terrible.

'Shad, I don't blame you. Maybe I should have made up something. If I'd have said gun running or narcotics or something, you'd have been with me all the way. Just because I tell you this little true story, corny, if you like, you don't go for it.'

He wasn't certain. Peering at me shrewdly he said : 'I'm good with names. Comes from this trade of mine. What would be the name of this farm-flower?'

I swallowed.

'Anthea Horan,' I told him.

'That's it. Out. If I'm not to be trusted with a simple missing person yarn, you can't be trusted with my files.'

'Shad, I swear it.'

Maybe my honest face changed his heart. Shaking his head sadly he moaned.

'I'm getting too old for the work. O.K., O.K. But if I find out you've been lying to me— Patsy.'

He didn't mean me. He was shouting for a girl outside. She came in on the run, ignoring me.

'Yes, Mr. Steiner? You have a story for me?'

He looked at her pityingly.

'Patsy, how many times do I have to tell you? You've been with us how long?'

She was a dark little thing, bouncing with get-up-and-go reporting fever.

'Almost six weeks, Mr. Steiner.'

'Almost six weeks. I was almost six years around the office before they trusted me with my first assignment. You know what it was?'

Her face fell as she nodded her head.

'It was a fire, wasn't it?'

'That's right. A one-alarm fire. They only sent me because they didn't have anybody else. When I got there, a patrolman had put it out with a bucket of water. One bucket. Now will you calm down and take Mr. Preston here down to the morgue. Talk to him. He's a very well-known citizen. We have a cabinet full of his little exploits down there.'

'Really?'

Now for the first time she could spare me a glance. Full of bright shining hope of future by-lines. As we opened the door to leave, Steiner called out :

'And Patsy . . .'

'Yessir.'

'. . . Nothing leaves the files. Mr. Preston is very welcome to look. That is all he's welcome to.'

I nodded my thanks for this expression of

29

brotherly trust, and we went out, heading down the steps into the depths of the building. Patsy was watching me covertly out of the corner of her eye. She'd probably learned not to take too literally everything her respected boss told her.

'First job?' I asked.

'Yes. Why yes it is. How'd you guess?'

'Just being sociable. You're taking up journalism as a career?'

'But of course. There's no other, you know. And I'm darned lucky to be working for Mr. Steiner too. He's the most.'

We were at the bottom now, among the familiar rows of file cabinets. I knew where to look. She scuttled along behind me saying in a surprised voice :

'Oh, you know your way around?'

'I ought to, after all these years.'

I started pulling open drawers, riffling through. Dan Crompton had been a good guesser. The Studio Six excitement had taken place five and a half years before. As I became absorbed in the clippings, Patsy went away and left me to it. As stories go it wasn't very exciting. The police had raided the place, making a number of arrests and confiscating photographic equipment and materials. They also took into care hundreds of so-called art poses and a collection of two-reel movies, The kind that get trotted out at stag dinners. The principal offenders were two men and a woman. The men were Robert H. Stone, 34, and Joseph Judson, 38. Both got four years. The woman was not in custody but her name was Clara Jean Dollery, age about 30. There were pictures of the men and I felt a small tingle when I saw Judson's face. He wasn't as handsome as I'd been given to understand, but there was no escaping the latin lover appearance. This could well be the Joseph Walstrom I was looking for. I studied his face carefully, and also that of his partner. There was no picture of the woman Dollery. Among the other accused there were no less than seven women, none of them named Anthea Horan. I wrote down everything carefully, wishing I could borrow the Judson and Stone photographs. Not that courtroom shots are very wonderful, and in any case they'd both be almost six years older now. I looked without much hope at the names of the seven women. They were all Chi-Chi this and Lulubelle that, and I was willing to bet none of their names was the one they were born with. In any case with dames of that kind, I wasn't going to be able to track down even one of them within two days, leave alone seven. So if Anthea Horan had graduated into that distinguished company, she may well be untraceable.

'Hey.'

A finger jabbed at my shoulder. I'd forgotten about Patsy.

'H'm?'

'Would you be Mark Preston?'

'I would. What of it?'

Her eyes sparkled.

'Boy, this is my day. I just looked you up. Mr. Steiner was right. We must have half a ton of paper about you. You seem to have a nose for murder, don't you?'

'No honey, I just have a nose for following facts and no more. Thanks for the hire of the hall.'

'Find anything?' she queried breathlessly.

'Yes. Just facts. Here.' I handed her the folder. 'You put it back. Then you can tell Mr. Steiner you're certain I didn't steal anything.'

Behind me the drawer slammed as I walked away.

'Mr. Preston,' and there she was again, bustling along behind.

'H'm?'

'Why don't you let me come with you? Honestly, I have to get close to some real crime. I wouldn't get in the way, really.' And she put a hand on my arm, 'I can be very good company if you happened to need any encouragement.'

I looked down into the eighteen-year-old face.

'Tell you what you do,' I suggested. 'Do you have a sister, say, ten years older than you?'

She bit her lip.

'There's Ellen,' she replied seriously. 'She's almost twenty-six. But I don't see—'

I patted the hand.

'When I get discouraged, you can be a real help. I'll come down here, you give me Ellen's number, I'll call her.'

She called me something she hadn't any business to have heard and flounced away.

I waved at Steiner through the glass door as I went out.

CHAPTER THREE

I went back to the office. It was almost seven, and La Digby had cleared up for the night. There were no telephone messages. Going through to my own office I helped myself to some iced water, then parked behind the desk and put through a call to the Fourth Precinct. I wanted Ben Fawcett of the Fraud Squad, but they told me he wasn't due for duty until nine o'clock. I hung around for an hour, toying with the few pieces of information I had, and making little of them. At eight I thought I'd get along to see Ben, taking in one or two of the friendly neighborhood bars on the way.

It was almost dark outside. As I approached the Chev a man's voice said:

'Mr. Preston?'

I turned to see a pleasant-faced young man in a dark flannel suit. Behind him at the kerb I saw a police-type sedan.

'Yeah. I'm Preston.'

'Eldredge, Sixth Precinct. Like you to come along with us if you would.'

'What's it all about?' I wanted to know.

He shrugged and grinned.

'Don't ask me, Mr. Preston. I just collect the merchandise.'

It was on the tip of my tongue to ask if he had a warrant, but I checked myself. No point in upsetting the law. If I wanted a warrant they'd soon get one, and the subsequent interview would be less friendly. Decidedly.

'O.K.' I sighed. 'But I hope it won't take too long.'

He held open the rear door of the sedan and I stepped in. As I did so something crunched against the side of my head, and I stretched out painfully on the floor. I heard the door slam behind me as I lost consciousness.

Next thing I knew was a foot kicking at my ribs. It wasn't a hard kick, but a steady rhythm from a pointed leather toe, and I grunted with sudden pain as my mind cleared.

'He's coming around,' said somebody.

I tried to lift my head in the darkness but a foot was pressed hard against the back of my neck.

'This'll do.'

I realized I was still in the car as brakes were suddenly applied.

'Now you listen, Preston,' grated a voice.

34

'We're your buddies, got it?'

'With buddies like you, I don't need any enemies,' I gritted.

'Always with the mouth. I heard about that. Keep it shut if you don't want it full of leather.'

I did like the man said. Some people just say things, others do them. This guy, I knew, was a doer. A new voice said, from the darkness above me:

'Like the man told you, we're your friends pal. Believe it. We're giving you good advice, and for free. There's people want you knocked off, but we said no. Not this time. We'll kind of talk to him, we said, explain things. Then, if there's a next time, maybe we was wrong to be so nice. Got it?'

'I don't know what,' I began, but the foot on my neck shoved my nose into the floor matting.

'Your nose, it's too big. You're a kinda funny looking guy, seems to me. All nose and mouth. Stop poking into things, flapping your gums all over town. People don't like it.'

Breathing was becoming difficult, and all the dust in the State was filling my nostrils and mouth.

'That's it, pal. Say good night to the man.'

'Sure,' said another voice.

Something hard swished past my ear and slammed against my head. I tried another mouthful of the matting. I seemed to feel other, lesser pains and there was a lot of

35

distant noise. After that I passed out.

The first thing I established was that I was no longer in a car. No car, however careless the owner, has grass growing inside it. Feeling carefully around with my fingers, I decided I was lying on the ground. A gentle lift of the head told me there was no foot pressing against it. Gingerly I looked up, and something hot banged inside my skull. After a minute or two of grunting and heaving, I managed to achieve a sitting position. My eyes accustomed themselves gradually to the gloom, and I could see I was sitting at the side of a highway. An unlighted highway. Fishing in my pockets I dug out a pack of Old Favorites, found one that wasn't bent in half and put a shaky flame to it. I puffed sadly at the weed wondering how many days or hours had passed. It was then I had the first sign of dawning intelligence, and remembered I owned a watch. According to the watch it was eight forty and I thought it must have stopped. But the steady ticking told me the watch was right, and I was wrong. A lot had happened in forty minutes. And the annoying thing, I hadn't the remotest idea who had done this to me, or why. Correction, I had to assume the why was connected with Anthea Horan, but a lot of people were involved already, and it could be to do with any one of them. Or rather, what I'm trying to think is . . .

I gave that up in disgust. Thinking is for clear-headed people. People who do not have little red men with hammers zooming around the inside of their cranium. In the distance, lights twinkled and moved. Could be headlamps. My first reaction was that my new buddies were on their way back with more advice. I looked around in panic for somewhere to hide, and the bare scrubland looked back at me. It was ridiculous anyway. Those guys had said what they wanted to say first time around. They weren't the kind to forget anything.

Clambering to my feet, I wavered out into the middle of the road, facing the oncoming lights. The beam picked up and became dazzling, and for a moment I thought the guy wasn't going to stop. Then, as I was getting ready to fall out of the way, brakes screeched, and a heavy truck pulled up a few feet in front of me.

'Ya wanta get killed? What kinda nut are ya?'

I grinned with relief at the rasping voice and stumbled towards it. A door slammed, and a husky character jumped down in front of me.

'Say, you look like you bin in one accident already.'

'Sort of,' I croaked. 'Where is this place?'

'You mean you don't know? You drunk, maybe?'

'Please,' I begged. 'Just tell me where we are.'

'You say so,' he shrugged. 'We're six miles

37

out of Monkton City. You know where that is?'

I felt relief flooding over me.

'Sure. Sure, I know it. Will you take me there?'

He shook his head, jerking it towards the rear.

'Sorry bud, I just come from there. Heading home for Corona. Take you there if you want.'

'No thanks. You'd enjoy the ride home better with an extra ten bucks in your pocket,' I pointed out.

'I don't know,' he muttered. 'Gettin kinda late. You mean it, about the ten?'

'I mean it.'

He had to help me up into the high cab, slamming the door to be sure I didn't fall out. Then he jumped up beside me, and began to swing the big wagon in a wide arc.

'What happened back there?' he wondered. 'I didn't see no car. Oh, I get it. Looks to me like you got tooken out there for a workout. That about it?'

'That's about it.'

He spat cheerfully out of the window.

'How many of 'em was there?'

'Three, I think. Could have been four.'

'Dirty bums. Ya want I should take ya to the cops?'

'No,' I said quickly. Too quickly. He stared at me with suspicion. I added, 'No, that wouldn't do at all. It was a family matter. You understand.'

38

His face cleared immediately.

'Oh, family trouble. That's different. I got plenty dose myself. Ya sure as hell don't want no cops messing in family business. Like I always say, we didn't have no families, there wouldn't be no war. People has to have wars every now and then, get some of the families out of the way.'

Quite relaxed now that he completely understood what had happened, he settled back at the wheel and regaled me with the first few chapters of a family history which I was certain he could have kept up all the way down to Mexico. It was lucky for me, I only had a few miles of it, although I would have liked to know what finally became of his wife's cousin Ham.

He dropped at the entrance to Parkside Towers. Till that moment I hadn't given it a thought, but I was relieved to find the goons hadn't helped themselves to my billfold. We parted good friends, and I shambled up to my apartment to get cleaned up. Twenty minutes and two Scotches later, I was back outside. My outward appearance was greatly improved by some fresh linen and a different suit of clothes. I even felt better inside after dunking my head in iced water a few times, but there was still an insistent thudding every four seconds at the base of my skull. No phoney policeman prevented me from getting into my car this time. When I walked into the headquarters of the Fourth Precinct, it was nine forty-five.

The desk sergeant was a new face. He looked at me incuriously as I walked up to him.

'Something I can do for you?'

'Like to see Sergeant Fawcett. I left a message I'd be coming in. Name of Preston.'

'Just a minute.'

He picked up a phone and dialled.

'Ben? Got a visitor, name of Preston. You will? Right.' He put down the phone and nodded to me. 'Take that first door on the left. The sergeant'll meet you.'

I thanked him and went through the door into a long low room. This was the duty squad room, where the squeals came in, and an endless army of people with information, people without information. People with missing husbands, cars, dogs. Old ladies who are certain the man next door was burying his wife during the night. Youths with flick knives and sullen expressions. Girls with dope in their handbags, and distraught parents on either side. Ladies from the country clubs with missing furs, ladies from the sidewalks with missing morals. The unceasing ebb and flow of troubles big and small, real and imagined, which is the normal run of business for the duty officer. The place was a subdued hubbub of telephones, interviews and cross-examinations. From a door at the side Ben Fawcett stuck out his head.

'Hallo Ben,' I held out my hand.

'Will it take long? I have a little surprise planned for a few friends at eleven.'

Which was going to be bad news for somebody. I squeezed past the desk in the box-sized office and parked in the only spare chair.

'Shouldn't take more than a few minutes,' I promised. 'I'm trying to find a missing girl, or I should say woman.'

'Well, which is it?'

'Both. She was a girl when she went missing, but it was fourteen years ago.'

He nodded, leaning back in his chair at a dangerous angle.

'She's a big girl now. But we don't run missing persons here—'

'Right. I know that. The way to this girl seems to be by way of an old customer of yours. Joseph Judson.'

I looked at him expectantly. He sat very quietly, inspecting the ceiling. Finally he shook his head.

'Sorry. Nothing. What was the pinch?'

'Stag movies, art photographs, outfit named Studio Six.'

He looked even more puzzled.

'That would be mine all right, but nothing happens. When was this vile villain apprehended?'

'Five and a half years ago. I've just been reading the story in old copies of the *Globe.*'

'Five and a half, that would be—yes.' He

41

clicked his fingers. 'Brother you had me worried there. I thought my amazing and infallible brain had let me down. But not so. In those days, this was only the Fraud Detail. We didn't have Morals lumped on to us until four years ago. The mystery is solved. Don't worry, the file will tell all.'

He pressed down a key and talked to somebody called Dave. Within minutes the door opened and a young policeman appeared with a thin buff folder under his arm. He didn't offer it to Fawcett. Instead he held out a small piece of paper.

'Will you sign, sergeant?'

Fawcett took the chit, glared at the newcomer, and scribbled his name. Then he was allowed to have the file. When the door closed he said:

'I swear, Preston, ever since the captain read some dreary book called Modern Police Forces of the World or something, we have to sign everytime we want the john.'

Muttering to himself he opened the folder and sifted quickly through it.

'Yup,' he announced. 'All here. The way a file ought to be, or nearly. Original squeal, enquiries, statements, prosecution, jail. Real tidy. But why do we need three pictures of each suspect?'

'Isn't that the way a modern police force file ought to be?'

I looked at him with a straight face and got

a scowl in return.

'If you want cooperation,' he suggested, 'cut out those terrible jokes.'

'Deal. Why did you say the file was only nearly perfect?'

'The woman,' he tapped at the papers. 'This Clara Jean Dollery was never caught. Still Judson is your man isn't he? Got four years at the country club. Lost a little remission over a brawl in the pen, got out two years ago.'

'Any idea where he is now?'

'No. He seems to have gone out of sight. Sorry, I can't help you.'

Another blank wall at the end of the street. I sighed.

'Not my lucky night. How about the other man er—' I looked at my scribbled notes— 'Stone. He missing too?'

He looked down again.

'No. Stone got maximum remission, came out six months before Judson. Don't know whether I should tell you about Stone.'

'Come on, be nice. He's my last hope, just about. If he can tell me where to find Judson—'

'If he can and will tell you,' corrected Fawcett.

'—All right, agreed. But I won't even get a refusal if I don't get to ask him,' I pointed out.

The sergeant leaned back again, thinking.

'You know what I'm wondering? I'm wondering whether you're telling me the truth.'

43

'Huh? I don't understand. Why wouldn't I?'

'How would I know? You imitation policemen can be very devious characters when you want.'

'Maybe,' I said non-committally. 'But why would I want to be? This case is so old it's got moss all over it.'

'True. All right Preston, I'll tell you what I'm going to do, fool that I am. I'm going to trust you.'

About to make a smart retort, I bit it through half-way and it died in my throat.

'Now listen,' and he pointed a gnarled finger at me. 'I'm telling you this because I don't want you upsetting a lot of delicate groundwork which is in progress. Start stamping your big feet around too much and you might spoil a very intricate investigation. As you can imagine, I'd be kind of resentful if you did.'

I leaned forward seriously, resting my elbows on the desk.

'You're not telling me you're doing something new about the case after all these years. I can stand a certain amount of coincidence, but that would be a little strong to swallow.'

Ben shook his head, looked at me as if wondering whether to go back on what he'd said.

'It isn't that. As you say this stuff is dead history. It's the man Stone. We're interested in him for quite different reasons. Nothing to do with this at all. But if you go round there, making him nervous, it could make him that bit extra careful, just when we want him careless.'

'I'll be like a cat walking on hot bricks,' I guaranteed. 'You know, delicate. Anyway, if there's genuinely no connection, I don't see what harm I can do. I'm just a private nose, I don't represent the forces of law and order, and he'll know it.'

'Yes, that's true,' assented Fawcett. 'That's really the point that decided me to let you have the dope. But watch it, will you?'

'Will do. Where can I find him?'

'Not far from here. You know a sewer called the Red Pig?'

'These places open and fold like musicals. What was it called before?'

'Lemme see. Yes, I have it. The Cash Register, that was it.'

I knew it now. One of the traps along Conquest Street. The Cash Register closed its doors on the grateful public several months back. One week later it was opened again, and I'd forgotten the new name till Fawcett reminded me. That was all that was new, the name. Everything else was the same, the décor, the furniture, the price of the drinks. It was the normal hazard on Conquest.

'What does he do at this place?' I queried.

'He's the boss. Or so he says. At least he sits

45

in the manager's office telling everyone what to do. Personally I have my own views about it. I think there's somebody behind him, somebody big.'

'But you're not going to tell me who the somebody is.'

He glared at me suspiciously.

'Correct. And why would you want to know? What's that got to do with a missing dame from way back?'

'Probably nothing,' I agreed. 'But you know how I never turn down any bits of information which are offered.'

'There's no more on offer,' grunted Fawcett.

'One thing,' I began hesitantly. 'You mention there were three photographs of Judson. You can't have a real need for three after all this time.'

'And?'

'And it would be a big help to me when I'm talking to people. Names can be changed, faces come a little more endurable.'

'You have your nerve. This here is confidential police information. How would it be if we started handing it over to everybody who felt like walking into the office?'

'Aw, come on Ben. Don't kid me. What can be confidential about a picture of a con. The guy was in every newspaper in the State at the time.'

He fidgeted, tapping at the file.

'Yeah. Well. These things cost money. Tell

you what, slip five bucks into the Police Benefit box at the desk on your way out.'

He lifted out one of the pictures and handed it across. I got up from the chair.

'Well thanks, Ben. This is a real help. I mean it.'

'So you should. If you happen to notice anything round that way, anything you think might interest a tired old police officer, you'll drop it my way, doubtless?'

'Doubtless.'

I thanked him again and went out. In the big office an elderly woman was being calmed down by two sweating guardians of the peace. I gathered, as I slipped gratefully past, that Pussy had never been out of the house at night before.

CHAPTER FOUR

By ten o'clock at night, Conquest Street is beginning to pick up its full tempo. Canned music blares raucously from a hundred fronts, while riotous neon signs flicker on and off the varied attractions available to the fortunate public. The Naughty Parlor—Joe's Jazz—Blue Midnight—Girls—Win a Pot—Gents only— The Ball Game—Girls—For Art's Sake— Hawaii Heaven. Groups of men saunter along, talking loudly and laughing too much. Young couples stroll with linked arms, oblivious to the confusion around them. The occasional early drunk staggers happily towards some dark spot where the lurking muggers will leave him with nothing but his teeth, and not even those if he tries to argue about it. Hookers parade brassily through the throng, muttering their invitations to anyone who hesitates. Here and there, a solitary man hurries past, head tucked down so that nobody can say later they saw him on Conquest Street. Everybody, from the mayor down, agrees that something has to be done about the eighty-block run, which is like an open wound on the city's body. Occasionally some organization sponsors a morals committee to report the facts. They are not hard to find, and the committee conclusions are quickly reached. Invariably, they call for immediate public action, a united front against the sin and corruption, a rooting out of evil. Conquest merely shrugs, and turns the music up a little louder. The simple fact is that Conquest Street would wither and die within a week, without any action by committees, without a single speech by a crusader. All it takes is for the money to stop rolling in. If the indignant public, the affronted citizens, took one easy step, the problem would be solved for ever. Because Conquest needs money, the way a junkie needs a fix. Without it, no wheels turn, no one operates. So all that needs to be done, is for the people to stay away. It's that simple. If they stayed home, and their money with them. Conquest would cease to exist. But it's a significant fact that no matter how affronted they may be, no matter how much they deprecate the existence of the place, they do not take that one short step which will solve the problem. There has to be a moral in there some place.

I strolled along, wishing somebody could tone down the noise and the color till my head stopped banging. The Red Pig was half-way down the street, and there was plenty to take in on the way. I found it necessary to stop at least twice, to study the large glossy photographs of large glossy females who were guaranteed to be appearing within. Eventually I managed to reach the place I wanted, without having been diverted to other attractions en route. No one could say the Red Pig was plushy from outside. Little more than a doorway, it had a small sign of a Disney-type pig playing a trombone. That was all, no name, no advertising. You could easily miss the place if you didn't happen to know what you were looking for. I pushed open the door and found myself in a narrow passage with, of all things, carpet on the floor. This is not usual in the average bar along that particular section. At the end, the passage turned left, and stairs led downward. As I descended I saw a table, and behind that a man in a tuxedo watching me approach. In front of him was a large book.

'Evening,' he said. 'Are you a member?'

I looked at him blankly. He was thirty, and large but soft with it. The hands fingering at the book had never laid eyes on a day's work.

'Member?' I echoed. 'Member of what?'

His smile became very slightly stiff.

'Of the club,' he informed me.

'This is a club?'

'Really,' he remonstrated. 'We're not going to get anywhere if you just repeat everything I say.'

'That's reasonable,' I conceded. 'Tell you what we'll do, you say something that makes sense, and I won't repeat it.'

The smile was now no more than a travesty.

'I'm sorry, I think you must be drunk. Perhaps you will leave.'

'Sure, after I've been inside.'

I went to move past the table, but he stepped smoothly in front of me.

'I'm sorry,' he said definitely. 'You can't go in.'

'Wrong,' I told him. 'I am going in. Lay a finger on me, and I'll book you for assault.'

Sensing that I wasn't going to hit him back, he became more aggressive. Poking at me with a chubby forefinger, he said :

'That's all. Out.'

'Behave yourself,' I tutted. 'Go tell Stone I'm here.'

The forefinger wavered and went away.

'Mr. Stone?'

50

'And don't repeat everything I say,' I mimicked. 'Just tell him.'

He was no longer certain.

'What do you want him for?'

'That's my business. And his. How would it be if every doorkeeper in town knew all his business? He wouldn't like it.'

'Wait here.'

He pulled a black velvet curtain to one side. I caught a quick glimpse of a soft-lit interior before the curtain fell back in place. The soft man wasn't away for long. Soon the curtain moved again and he beckoned me.

'This way.'

I went through. The room wasn't very big, not as big as I recalled from the days when the place was called The Cash Register. In a corner an overhead blue spot fell on a man hunched lovingly over a piano keyboard. He was almost stroking the keys, and they responded by purring out some old Rodgers and Hart, in a way that made me regret I couldn't listen longer.

We walked along one side to where a black door carried the loving message, Positively No Admittance. The big man knocked, then opened the door and motioned me inside. The room seemed to be in darkness, but as the door closed lights came on automatically. I found myself standing side on to a desk, and turning, saw a man sitting watching me. He was a thick set man, with heavy jowls from

51

which he had difficulty in scraping the blue whiskers at least twice a day.

'Who are you?' he demanded.

The voice lacked lyrical quality. In fact it sounded like the kind of noise you hear in a sheet metal shop.

'You first. Mr. Stone?'

'I'm Stone,' he acknowledged. 'I like to know who I'm throwing out of my place.'

I held up a hand of peace.

'My name is Preston, and there's no need for you and me to get off on the wrong foot, Stone. That guy outside, he's going to get you and your place in trouble, you don't watch out.'

The black eyes narrowed.

'Trouble? What kind trouble?'

'The worst kind. Law trouble. He's jazzing it up out there in a most illegal fashion.'

'Illegal?' From the way he said it, Stone evidently thought I was crazy. 'Illegal? Listen man, this is the most legal place on the whole street. You won't find a thing wrong out there. Twenty cops couldn't find a thing wrong out there.'

'Maybe. I'm talking about the entrance. According to the cream-puff, you have to be a member to get in here.'

'Correct. This is a private club,' he affirmed.

'Wrong. This is a public place. There's nothing outside says it's private. You want to run a private club, that's fine with the law. But there has to be a sign outside says so. You don't have one. There's a whole flock of law on the subject, federal, state and city. It's a great big bag of confusion, and you want to do yourself a favor, have some lawyer run it over for you.'

Some of the confidence left his eyes.

'That's on the level? I been here a long time, nobody ever tried to pull this one on me before.'

'You've been lucky,' I assured him. 'But don't worry, I'm not going to tell anybody. Not why I came.'

'All right,' he sighed. 'I guess you done me some kind of favor. I'll get a sign. Just what did you come for?'

There was a low comfortable-looking chair opposite the desk. Now that we'd gone past the stage where I was about to get the heave, I stretched out on it. My head was level with a large glossy picture of a woman's face, a beautiful woman's face. Stone turned it away from me irritably.

'I'm looking for somebody. Old friend of yours. Joe Judson.'

Any softening of his features had disappeared again.

'I don't know anybody by that name.'

'Oh pshaw,' I tutted. 'You have a bad memory. You want me to run over the details?'

He sat silent, examining his thick fingers.

'I think you'd better. And just watch what

53

you say,' he said finally.

'All right. You're Robert M. Stone. You and Joe Judson ran a place called Studio Six, that was years back. You did some bad things, you and Joe, and the law put you away. That's not important to me, I didn't come here to rake over all those dead leaves. They let you loose two and a half years ago. Joe wasn't so lucky, they couldn't bear to part with him for a further six months. All I want to know is, where do I find him?'

Again he studied his fingers. He seemed to think they were so interesting I took a quick peek at them myself, in case they were turning green or something.

'What makes you think I know where he is? I didn't have nothing to do with Joe after he came out. What do you want him for?'

'I guess there's no harm in telling you that. I'm not really interested in Joe at all. Nor you, believe me. I'm looking for a girl who came to this city with Joe fourteen years ago.'

For once he stopped looking at his hands long enough to shoot a glance across at me.

'Fourteen—you have to be kidding.'

'No, I don't have to be. In fact I'm not.'

He laughed, a short dry rasp.

'Man, fourteen years is a lifetime. Why I didn't even know the guy myself back then. And if you imagine for one minute Joe Judson would remember a dame more than fourteen days, you don't know much about him. Listen, that guy had dames the way other people have socks. You don't look so dumb to me. You really think you have a chance to locate this mouse? She's probably somebody's grandmother by this time.'

I didn't need Stone to tell me what I was up against.

'I know all that,' I assured him. 'And I'm not going to make a lot of progress till I find Judson. Now, how about it?'

'I already told you. I didn't have any part of him after—'

'Nobody said you did,' I pointed out. 'But don't try to tell me he didn't come to look you up after he got out. There'd be things to clear up between you. He'd have to come.'

'Sure, I saw him a coupla times. And that was that.'

'What became of him?' I persisted.

'Search me. Like you said, we had a coupla things to talk over. I let him have some dough—'

'Why? You don't look like no fairy godmother from here.'

'Because he had it coming. Some of that stuff we were operating before the law came was worth money. Joe was entitled to a share. He took it and blew.'

'And you don't know where.'

'Right.'

'When was this?'

'Let's see, it all happened within weeks of

him getting out of jail. Yeah, it must be two years since I saw him.'

I wasn't going to get any more. The annoying thing was, I couldn't be certain Stone wasn't telling the truth. I wanted him to be lying, but inside I knew that was because he was my only hope of a lead to Judson. I got up.

'Well, I guess I'm wasting my time. Give my love to Clara Jean.'

He was on his feet in a flash. As he did so a livid scar showed suddenly on his face. I hadn't noticed it earlier owing to the poor light, but the rush of angry blood lit it up like a beacon. His voice was very soft. And very dangerous, when he said :

'You had better go now. When you get outside, stay there. Don't come pushing your dirty nose down here again, or I'll chop it off for you. I don't like cops too well, but private cops stink. You get moving now, right now. Don't stop till you're up on the street.'

'Nice talking with you,' I assured him.

The lights in the room switched out as I opened the door. Then I was edging my way along the dark wall again, catching another few melodic bars from the man under the spotlight. Outside in the hall, the big soft man looked up in surprise as I approached.

'Been having a lovely chat with your boss,' I told him gaily. 'Guess what? He's going to fire you.'

He stared at me, puzzlement on the flabby

face, as I made my way back up to the tinselled splendors of Conquest Street. Directly opposite the Red Pig was a pool-room. I went over there and leaned up against the wall. Funny thing about pool-rooms, you can lean or stand outside them for hours on end, and nobody even notices. In fact it's so much a part of the scene, people tend to stare if there isn't anyone lounging around outside. Somebody once told me of a pool-room in his home town where the proprietor used to get so worried if there weren't any loiterers, he'd go out and hire some by the hour.

From where I was I could see the entrance to the Red Pig quite clearly, and also the narrow passage at the side which led to the rear entrance. If there was still a rear entrance. I didn't know whether Stone could help me find Judson or not, but one thing was certain, he knew about me. He'd called me a private cop, and I hadn't told him that. If I'd been lucky enough to upset him or worry him he might just come dashing out to go and tell somebody. Maybe he'd lead me straight to Joe Judson. I could see it all. I'd walk right in on them. Stone, Judson and poor Anthea, chained to the wall where the fiendish pair had enslaved her these fourteen years. No, that wouldn't work out. They'd have had to have someone feed her while they were filling in time up at the big house.

I stuck it out for thirty useless minutes,

dropped my second butt on the ground and stomped it out. If I'd had any effect at all on Stone, it had been something he could take care of on the telephone. Turning to go, I stopped as someone walked past the brilliant entrance of the girlie show next to the place I was watching. It was the man who called himself Eldridge, the one who suckered me into that police-looking car earlier. I made to dash across the street but a cruising blue-top got in the way. After it passed I was in time to see him turn into the crack in the buildings which led to the rear of the Red Pig.

My sudden anger cooled by the encounter with the cab, I walked swiftly across and looked down the narrow gap. I was just in time to see light flood out into the murk, illuminating the imitation police officer as he stepped inside. Waiting for the door to close behind him, I walked silently to the doorway. It was like a stage door in prohibition days, iron bound and with solid steel rivets all around the outside. It was also firmly locked. Well, maybe that was enough for tonight. Even if I got in, and started tossing muscle around, it wouldn't prove anything. Guys like that weren't going to bust out crying and hand over Anthea's address. Even supposing they knew it. Besides, as things were, I had a slight edge. I knew there was a connection between Stone and the guys who had given me a light workout. On top of that, they weren't aware I knew it.

It was nearly midnight, and I was beginning to feel weary now, from the effects of that little discussion with Eldridge and his friends.

After all, I reasoned, I hadn't done too badly in a few hours. There wasn't anything of much value I could do at that hour. And even a private buzzer is entitled to some sleep occasionally. That, at least, was what I thought.

CHAPTER FIVE

I closed the door of my apartment and yawned. On the short ride back my thinking had become a little clearer. Thinking I hadn't made too bad a stab at the assignment, that was so much hogwash designed as a conscience salver, so I could get to bed. What had I really accomplished, when you boiled it right down? Nothing. I was no nearer Anthea Horan now than the moment her sister walked into the office.

The thought of her sister made me grin. I wondered what she would say, back there in the farmhouse, if she knew the kind of places her little enquiries had taken me. Not to mention some of the lovely people I'd talked with.

Tossing my coat on a chair, I broke out a

can of beer and sat down to watch a late newscast before hitting the sack. There wasn't anything worrying enough to keep me awake all night. I swallowed the last of the beer and switched out. I made it as far as the door of the bedroom before the phone started hollering. Grumpily, I padded across to the thing.

'Well?'

Sam Thompson's voice was indignant.

'Where've you been? Listen, this is the fifth time I called you—'

'So put it on the account. What's new? Did you lose him?'

His voice was guarded.

'Well, kind of. In a manner of speaking. Look, you know the Bells are Ringing?'

'What's that, a song?'

'It's a bar, Preston, a bar. On Pioneer Street. Half a block away from that other place where we were. You remember.'

'Bar?' I snorted. 'I'm not paying you to hang around bars. So help me Sam—'

'Quit busting your girdle and listen. This phone is kind of public, I can't say too much. But I think you better get down here.'

'Get? Do you know what time it is?'

'I have twelve thirty. What do you make it?'

I knew it was useless. If Thompson wanted me, he wanted me. To argue about it was a waste of time. And if I didn't go, I might miss the one thing which could prove useful. Groaning and complaining every step of the way, I agreed to see him in twenty minutes.

Five minutes later I was heading back the way I'd recently come. If only I'd known earlier where to find Thompson, I could have walked it within minutes from the Red Pig. I stopped the car fifty yards from the place with the optimistic title, and carefully locked it. Then on reflection, I went all round it a second time, making double sure. On Pioneer Street at night a man has to make double sure of everything. Anything movable will be moved, by the unseen army of petty thieves who infest the quarter.

The outside of the Bells are Ringing conveyed an impression of inner gloom and squalor. The interior confirmed that impression, in spades. It was a strictly-for-drinking bar, bare wooden tables, hard chairs, wooden floor. There wasn't any conversation going on. People had come to drink, and talking would only hold up the action. For the most part they sat in solitary and gloomy silence, working their way through the glasses, each man to a pre-determined pattern of his own. To my surprise, Thompson was at the far end of a row from the bar. It was unlike him to expose himself to a lot of legwork each time he needed a refill.

When he saw me some of the misery went out of his face. Not much. I looked at his half-empty glass.

'What is that stuff?'

61

'They made a mistake. I asked for Scotch. This here is embalming fluid.'

'Glad you told me.'

Some bars you visit the jockey keeps a baseball bat in handy reach under the counter. Not so in the Bells are Ringing. Maybe the barman feels there's no time for all that leaning down. He has his bat resting on a couple of brackets at hand level. And not just any old stick, either. This one was fancied up with metal bindings at the business end. The bartender didn't like me. He stared at my face so he'd remember it.

'You want what?'

I ran my eyes over the dirty shelves, settled for two cans of imported lager. One thing about cans, no matter where you put them. The beer inside stays clean. He overcharged me, waited to see if I'd complain, but all I wanted was to talk to Thompson in peace.

I carted my new valuables back to the table.

'This had better be good,' I warned Thompson. 'It was your idea to visit this gay Hawaiian paradise. What'd you find out?'

'I fouled it up,' he muttered mournfully.

'Great. You could've told me that on the phone. If you've dragged me down here—'

'Wait. Will you please wait, and listen.'

He turned and studied the people nearest to us to see whether they were taking any interest. They weren't, but nevertheless he dropped his voice to little more than a croaked whisper.

'After you left me, I kept tabs on that place. Nothing happened for about an hour. Then that guy you mentioned, he came out. He was alone, and he was in a hurry. He went to the Rochdale Arms Apartments on Crane Street. You know it?'

I knew it. A crumbling firetrap where the police make a casual visit any time business is slow. They can always rely on finding at least one Navy deserter, somebody on the run, somebody with a supply of heroin under his pillow. If it's a good day for the law they may also net one or two in illegal possession of firearms, and somebody contributing to the deliquency of a minor. Whatever they turn up, there is always enough business to fill a few empty cells.

'And then?' I prompted.

'Like I said, the guy went in. I figured maybe he was visiting a friend and I also figured you might care to know who that friend was. He went to an apartment on the second floor, and it must be his own pad, because he had a key.'

'That doesn't follow,' I objected.

'Are you gonna let me tell you this story or not?' he demanded.

'All right, but get to the facts will you?'

He glared at me, sipped noisily at his beer.

'Like I was saying, I figured the guy was home. But just to be sure, I took a stroll up the fire escape and peeked in the window. It's just a one-room flop, and the man was alone. But he didn't strike me as the kind of guy to be catching an early night, so I thought maybe he was waiting for somebody. I couldn't spend hours on the fire escape, so I went back out front and watched from there. People came and went, quite a lot of people, and that's when I realized I was wasting my time. I couldn't identify half of these guys, and I hadn't any way of knowing which of them was for Tuborg, if any, It seemed to me there wasn't much point in spending any more of your money. But I thought I'd give it one last try before I gave up. So I gave the fire escape another play. You know, there was just a chance he might have somebody with him. There wasn't. But he'd had a visitor all right. Maybe two. They beat hell out of him and left him on the floor.'

He stopped talking and looked at me enquiringly.

'And that's all? You didn't get a look at who it could have been?'

'Who knows? There were guys in and out the whole time. Could have been any of them.'

'H'm.'

I pushed an Old Favorite into my face. Sam Thompson leaned over and extracted one. Nobody asked him.

'Help yourself,' I grunted.

'Thanks.'

He took two more and poked them in a pocket.

'Did you happen to notice any special cars calling? In particular, was there a dark sedan, you know the type the police use for their little private calls?'

He looked at me, pained.

'If there was anything like that, don't you think I'd have told you?'

'H'm. So what's the idea bringing me out in the cold night air? I imagine you could have told me all this over the phone?'

'Sure. But I thought you might want to do something about it. Like you and I go round to the Rochdale for example.'

I dragged smoke down where it would do the most harm.

'What for? You think we ought to give the guy medical attention?'

'My, we are sarcastic tonight. No, I was thinking something quite the opposite. Some people went to a lot of trouble to soften up this friend of yours. Seems a pity to let it go to waste. Struck me you might like to pay him a little visit. The condition he's in isn't about to make him love his nice friends, whoever they were. He's also in no frame of mind to be looking for another work out. Way I see it, the guy is a set-up for anybody who may want to ask him a few questions.'

Thompson was right of course. If I'd been at my best, he wouldn't have needed to spell it out for me that way.

'You're right. Let's go see him.'

Crane Street is at the lower end of Conquest, not more than a couple of blocks from where we were on Pioneer Street. I try to avoid Crane as much as possible, because I don't care for memories of that kind. It was where I started out on my star-studded career as a p.i. I lounged around down there a long time. All I had was a sign, and a bed, and a drawer full of bills. It seemed like a long time ago, now, but I still get the creeps whenever I visit the place, and marvel at the younger men who could stand it.

It had been a year or two since I'd seen the Rochdale Arms Apartments, and the place hadn't improved with age. We entered a grimy enclosure that passed for a hallway. Thompson poked at my arm and pointed upwards. We trod up the steep narrow stairs in silence, him leading. Upstairs he paused outside a door, listening. After a minute or so he nodded and tried the handle. The door opened with a faint protest and we went in. The light was on, and the first thing I saw was the fat man named Tuborg. He was lying, half on his face, with his knees pulled up tight into his middle. Somebody had stuck a foot of plaster across his eyes. I checked his heart quickly and was relieved to feel the steady pumping. He was lucky to be alive after the shellacking he'd had. His face was bruised and bloody, and where the dirty shirt had been ripped open there were blue and red weals in all directions.

'Snap it up Tuborg,' I encouraged.

Nothing happened. The man was out cold. Thompson scratched an ear.

'He ain't much use to you like this,' he mumbled.

I had an idea. It wasn't very pretty, but it looked as though I was mixed up in something where the only thing that mattered was results.

'Sam we're going to ask this guy a few questions. He won't even know what day it is if we bring him round. With that stuff over his eyes, we might be able to persuade him we're the people who did this. There's a snag. He knows my voice, so you'll have to ask the questions.'

'Me? I don't even know what this is all about,' he protested. I ran through my scene at the Four Horsemen, told Sam I was trying to find a man named Judson. There was also a Stone involved, who might very well be the guy who sent the gorillas after Tuborg.

'That would make him Mr. Stone for the purpose of these enquiries,' Sam pointed out.

'Good thinking. Now you have the idea. What we want to know is how much he told the man Preston about those people, and what happened long ago. Kabish?'

'I gotcha. Well, let's get it over with, I can't say I relish the idea too well.'

I picked up an overturned chair, set it

straight. Then we each took a helping of the vast bundle known as Tubby Tuborg, and heaved and grunted it into place on the chair. There wasn't any water in the place, water not being a liquid Mr. Tuborg was too well acquainted with. So I patted gently at his cheeks, until after a while he stirred and moaned.

'Come on will ya?' I grated.

He mumbled something I couldn't catch. I grabbed at his chin and jerked it upright, nodding to Thompson.

'Talk it up, fat boy,' Thompson said nastily, 'I can't hear you.'

'L-l-listen you guys, I swear, I told you all— all there is.'

'You're a liar,' Thompson told him. 'Let him have some more of the treatment.'

'No,' screamed Tuborg. 'No, please, please. Honest, I swear on my grave—'

'Don't rush things,' Thompson interrupted. 'Nobody mentioned any grave. Not yet. What'd you tell this snoop?'

'Nothing. I didn't tell him nothing, listen, it was just like I told you before.'

'I wasn't listening before. What happened? Or would you like another little workout?'

'No. Like I said, I'm in the Horsemen, just drinking is all. Just drinking. This guy comes in, makes a play for Mr. Dee. I get lending an ear, in case there's some loose change in it for me. That was all, just loose change.'

'You'll get some more loose teeth if you don't snap it up,' he was promised.

'I'm telling ya, I'm telling ya. This guy says he's looking for some chump dame who jumped the old ranch way back. I figure this is just a come-on. Anyway, Mr. Dee he gives the guy the air. I think maybe I can call on this character for a buck, so I follow him out. Then I find this dame went on the hoof a long time back, back in the old Studio Six days.'

'So you told him about the Studio?' said Thompson harshly.

'Gimme a break, will ya? I didn't tell him a thing, not a lousy thing. As soon as I realized which way this Preston was going, I clammed up. Ya gotta believe me.'

'No, we don't. That's exactly where you are wrong, fat man. All right, now what did you tell him about Mr. Stone?'

'Mr. Stone?' echoed Tuborg, very frightened. 'Ya think I'm crazy? I don't go around blabbing about Mr. Stone. Believe me, I wouldn't be that stupid.'

Thompson laughed, a short unpleasant bray.

'There ain't anybody as stupid as you. Right?'

'Right.'

'Then say so. There ain't anybody as stupid as you.'

Tuborg ran a thick pink tongue across trembling lips.

'There—there ain't anybody as stupid as me,' he muttered.

'Good. That's better. Now, how much dough this Preston give you to point the finger?'

Tuborg groaned.

'Whaddya want from me? I told ya ten times, the guy give me nothing.'

'Tell me again.'

'Nothing, I swear it. Search the place. You won't find more-n a dollar fifty in the whole lousy joint.'

'You,' said Thompson, pointing at me. 'Poke around.'

I trod on Tuborg's foot, not hard. It was just to remind him he wasn't alone with Thompson. Then I made a lot of noise, pulling out drawers and throwing stuff around. Somebody had done it all before me, so I knew there'd be nothing to find.

'Nothing,' I reported, in a deep voice.

'So you didn't take money. Maybe you told him for free,' persisted Thompson.

For a guy who didn't want the job, he was certainly making the best of it.

'What did you say about Judson?' was his next question.

'Nothing. I don't know nothing. Look, I ain't seen Joe in two years or more.'

'When was the last time?'

'Oh, I don't know. Just after he got sprung. I told you all this.'

70

Sam hit him lightly across the face, and the fat man cringed back in his chair.

'That's just to keep you awake. And don't talk back that way. Tell it again, about Judson.'

'Like I said,' stammered Tuborg. 'It was right after he got out. He came to the Horsemen, said he was looking for Mr. Stone. I told him I hadn't seen the man in years. He said he had some big deal brewing up over in Vale. We had a drink, maybe two. I ain't seen him from that day to this.'

'And that's all you told Preston?'

'I told him nothing.'

Thompson looked at me enquiringly, I shrugged my shoulders. We weren't going to get anything else of value from this quivering hulk. Thompson stuck a thick forefinger against Tuborg's throat.

'Now get this, fat boy. I hear tell there's people don't like this Preston. He ain't careful, he could have a terrible accident. If he does, you never heard of him. Got it?'

'Got it. Honest, believe me—'

'Shuddup. This accident he could have, they got a whole stock of the same kind of accidents. Could be you draw one too, unless you get a lot smarter than you are.'

'Please, gimme a break. I don't know this Preston. I never heard of him.'

'Keep thinking it.'

I pulled a ten from my pocket and waved it. Thompson said:

'Here's a sawbuck. Try to look neater, next time I see you.'

There was gratified surprise on Tuborg's face.

'Gee thanks.'

'Shuddup. It's not from me. I wouldn't give you the time of day. Just remember who your friends are. You know who to thank.'

Tuborg wagged his head up and down.

'Sure. You'll tell her I said thanks won't you? You'll do that please? I sure want her to know that.'

'Just keep your nose clean.'

I pointed to the door, and we left. The last thing I saw was Tuborg's face pointed fearfully towards the door. It was clear from his expression that he couldn't believe nobody was going to hurt him any more. We waited until we were half-way down the stairs before speaking.

'This here is a dirty business you're in Preston,' Thompson informed me coldly. 'Lucky for you I need the dough.'

'Don't read me sermons,' I snapped. 'I didn't really enjoy that any more than you did. But that guy knew the kind of people he was dealing with. And don't forget, he went to them to jack up the prices. If he'd taken the money I offered him today he wouldn't have collected those lumps.'

Thompson grunted something unintelligible. Outside, he squeezed five out of me on account and wandered off to find a quiet bar. I went home for the night, feeling a lot more hopeful than when I left it. Now I had places to go, people to find. The fat man had said Judson told him he was heading for Vale City. He also mentioned a woman, naturally with no name. In this business, any kind of information is better than none. The trouble is, the mind won't leave it alone, keeps nagging at it when a man ought to be getting his rest.

I lay in bed a long time before I finally drifted off.

CHAPTER SIX

I stayed in bed late the next morning, eventually stirred myself at nine thirty. While I was in the shower my stomach was muttering something about food. Then I realized I'd been so busy chasing around town on the Anthea thing, I hadn't had anything to eat since the previous noon. I wandered around, patting myself dry. The morning sun was coming through a window in a way that showed it meant business today. I broke out a fresh shirt, settled for a dark green knitted tie. Then I put on a fawn lightweight suit and admired myself in the mirror. Not bad, not bad at all, I congratulated. A guy can't be twenty-five his whole life, but some guys seem to head direct from twenty-five to advancing old age. The lucky ones, like me, have an in-between period. I mean looking at me this morning you'd think I was around thirty. No? Well? Well, say a young thirty-five. Still no? And was that a beginning of thickening there at the middle? I peered at it anxiously, decided it was the fault of the tailor. They don't make clothes the way they used to. Besides, they can't cut these lightweight materials the way they can the orthodox cloths. No, that was it, the suit was not hanging properly. I pulled and smoothed at it. There, that was better. Yes, I would think about thirty.

Reassured, I went out. Around the corner is a place where I sometimes take breakfast. The waitress is a stacked blonde, hardened by years of hand-dodging, but to me she's practically civil. She brought coffee and set it down in front of me.

'You eating today?'

'Why yes. let's see. I'll take scrambled eggs, bacon, toast.'

Was she looking at my waist, or just staring at the floor? 'No wait, leave the bacon. And just one piece of toast.'

Twenty minutes later I felt better, dawdling over a second cup of coffee and thinking about what I had to do. Regretfully, I stubbed out my Old Favorite and paid the girl. One thing I did not want to do was drive out on that desert highway in the mounting heat, but that was exactly what I must do.

Soon I was leaving the last of the split-level territory and heading out on that endless concrete strip. On either side now, the flat barren scrubland stretched away unbroken into the distance. The sun joyfully set about the business of turning my innocent car into a sweat box. I rolled down windows, switched on ventilating fans. They helped for a while, but soon I felt the circulating hot air was drying me out like some process of dehydration.

I was heading for Vale City, sixty miles from home, and a place I hadn't visited for some time. Vale is an interesting place, history-wise, and often visited by writers and other people interested in the pioneer days. Back then, the place was a kind of oasis.

There, by some geographical quirk, a large supply of clean water had been trapped. After a hundred and fifty miles of desert, and with plenty more to travel, the pioneers needed that water. And so, the creaking wagons would halt, the sweating horses head thankfully for their first fresh drink in days. There would be a letting-down atmosphere. After weeks of exposure and danger, the leaders of the train would vote a stopover of two or three days, to get their people back in good shape for the last stage of the trek. The name of the place needed no deliberation. This, after the wilderness, had to be the Vale of Eden. Some people decided to remain, and homestead within reach of the water. Others remained too, setting themselves up in business for the other trains which would follow. And so a community sprang up of tough serious people, who knew at first hand the needs of a homing wagon train. And after their own experiences, at earlier stages of the trail, they had very clear ideas as to just which services ought to be provided. Food, clothing, services for wagons and animals. These were the real needs. There would be no saloons, no girls, no gambling. They had seen too many frontier towns, knew the rapid decay which could set in once those particular needs were catered for. Knew how lawlessness would follow, bringing the get rich quick shysters and the gunfighters. Their own journey would have been that much easier had they not found it necessary to make periodic detours to avoid some free-shooting cluster of shacks. They reasoned that trade would follow order, and prosperity would follow trade. They were right too, and for half a century the place was a landmark on the trail, and a byword among the scouts and train leaders.

But a new generation came, and another. People who knew nothing of the desert, except that you had to watch out for those rattlers if you weren't wearing proper boots. They were impatient of the old traditions, and didn't know why they had to drive for miles in order to get a cool beer on a Saturday night. But the traditions held until after World War I. Then a small piece of legislation called Volstead blew the country apart, and Vale was not to be left out of it. Prohibition came to Vale City, and so did the bootleggers. It seemed that the crystal waters which had sustained those early travellers was also chemically possessed of a texture and flavor peculiarly suited to the bath-tub brew. It was the end of enforced abstention for the citizens of Vale. They had been in hiding for fifty years, building up the most almighty thirst, which they now proceeded to slake. They set about it in a fashion which astonished even the gun-toting brewers. One survey, carried out by prohibition agents, produced the interesting fact that there were more breweries, stills and bars in Vale City in proportion to the population than in any other community in the U.S. Not excluding even Chicago, Ill. From being the dryest town on record, Vale became within two short years the wettest. One newspaper even ran a serious campaign to get the name changed to Barville. Prohibition is long behind us, but even today Vale sustains more bars than any town its size.

A little over an hour after leaving Monkton, I rolled into the city. Police headquarters is on Saddler Street, named after the old-time leather worker who had been one of the original settlers. The man I wanted was one Lieutenant Franks, with whom I was acquainted slightly. A brown-shirted cop took me to an airy office on the first floor. On the door was the legend Murder Squad, E. Franks, Lieutenant. I went in and Franks got up from his desk, holding out a hand.

'Now I got you,' he greeted. 'I remembered the name, but I couldn't put a face on you.'

'How are you lieutenant.'

Franks is one of those cops I can talk to. A serious, fair-haired man about thirty years old, he is one of those lucky people who always contrives to look cool and neat even on a scorching day like today. I'd forgotten he didn't smoke, lit myself an Old Favorite as I sat down.

'Well, now, what can I do for you, Mr. Preston? I hope you're going to clear off half a dozen of my unsolved files?'

I grinned as I took papers from my pocket.

'I doubt that, lieutenant. In fact I'm probably on a wild goose chase. But I'm looking for a man who hasn't been seen for a couple of years. Last thing I can find out is he said he was coming this way.'

'Is that a picture of him?'

I handed over my picture of Judson. He took it, turned it over, and whistled.

'It says on here Monkton City P.D. Criminal Records Office. You working with the Monkton boys on this?'

'No,' I admitted. 'But I help them a little from time to time. They let me have the picture, kind of returning a favor.'

78

He liked that, I could see from the way he nodded his head. Now he was back to the shiny side, back to Judson's face. He held it away from him, cocked his head to one side.

'I don't think so,' he muttered. 'Don't think he's one of our local hoods. What do you have on him?'

'Ex-con,' I said briefly. 'He copped four years for making naughty pictures. Got out two years ago, said he was headed for Vale City. Since then, nothing.'

'Stag pictures uh? Those guys give me the creeps. Well I'm not about to take the stand on this, but I don't think I've seen him around. No trouble to ask the other squads though.'

'Thanks, I may ask you that. First, I was wondering if he might have come your way in the line of duty.'

He picked up the picture again and peered at it.

'You mean like feet first?'

I nodded.

'Look at it this way. A guy comes out of stir, heads for a strange town with an appointment. Maybe he has a share of something coming. Maybe somebody else has that share and takes off for the woods. But Judson knows where to find that somebody. When he turns up, asking for his cut, the somebody doesn't want to part with it. The somebody has kind of grown accustomed to thinking it his own property. So, when Judson gets tough about it, he gets the heave. Then he gets himself knocked off. It's happened before.'

'Sure, sure. It happened before,' agreed Franks doubtfully. 'It also happened, and much more frequently, that the ex con gets his cut, decides to start over somewhere new, takes the first train out.'

I knew that, too. But I didn't want to contemplate the possibility. Because for me, Vale City was the end of the line so far as Judson was concerned.

'Well,' I said regretfully, 'if you're quite sure—'

'Hold on,' the lieutenant held up a hand. 'Don't give up so easy. And I'm not quite sure. You don't expect me to take one look at a make on a guy and be quite sure? Wait.'

He picked up the black telephone and dialled three numbers.

'Filing? Franks. Look, I want pictures of all the homicides in the past two years. Keep the unsolved separate will you?'

He put down the phone and grinned. I grinned back. This was a man people always grinned at.

'Mighty good of you to take all this trouble, lieutenant. Might have taken me a month to cover all this ground you're dealing with in just a few minutes.'

'Think nothing of it,' he deprecated. 'And I'll tell you what else. If I can close any of those old files because of this little trip of yours, the beers are on me.'

While we sat around there glowing with mutual esteem, somebody put in some fast work in the filing department. Soon there were half-a-dozen thin folders in front of the policeman.

'H'm. Now let's see.'

He began to go carefully through the reports and photographs in front of him. Periodically, he would pause, stare, then pass on.

'Could be this one,' he said doubtfully, tapping at the papers.

I held out a hand and he passed over a photograph. It was a very good photograph, very clear. And my stomach marked time. The picture showed the naked body of a man, lying in some grass. He lay on his stomach, which made identification difficult. There was another factor which made it even harder. The man's head had been hacked off.

'Wow,' I murmured. 'Yes, I suppose we couldn't discount the possibility.'

'Right. Never discount any possibility,' agreed my host. 'We picked up that baby a mile from town, on some waste land. You're seeing all we ever found. No head, no clothes, nothing we could use for identification. Just one thing, you notice the hands?'

Except that they looked unnaturally flat and stiff, I couldn't see anything unusual about them.

'They seem very flat. Nothing else.'

'That's it,' he explained. 'We had to put 'em that way to get out whatever he was clutching. You know what he had? A silver dollar in each hand. Mean anything?'

'Sure.' I nodded. 'It's the ultimate sign of contempt. It's only used in gang killings. Haven't heard of it in years.'

'Neither had we. So, that's one possibility. Still, we'll check 'em all out.'

I gladly handed back the glossy picture. It wasn't my idea of light entertainment on a hot, sticky afternoon. Franks continued his methodical poring. Suddenly he stopped.

'Hey now, we could have a little something here.'

He lifted another photograph, and stared hard. Then he handed it to me.

'What do you think?'

I took it and steeled myself for another experience like the last. But this one was harmless. Except for a fixed expression on the face this man could have been alive. He was clean-shaven, and with startling white hair, although he looked no more than forty years old. I tried to imagine him with a moustache, and held my hand over the hair, looking quickly from the picture to the one of Judson I'd brought with me.

'I don't know,' I admitted. 'Could be. It certainly could be. But I couldn't be positive. What do you have about this one?'

He was reading quickly through the reports, and held up a hand for me to wait. Meantime I carried on studying the two pictures.

'At my age I should know better, but I'm practically excited,' Franks told me. 'The customer you're looking at was by the name of James Earnshaw. He had an address at 2727 Dunphy Apartments, on Hamilton Street L.A. We naturally contacted the department there. Here is a return report. It says "Deceased rented the apartment one week before your enquiry, paying one month's rent in advance. Cannot trace that he ever occupied the apartment. No one knows him." There are other bits of information, but they all add up to big fat zero.'

I wagged my head hopefully.

'Better and better. How did he happen to come your way, lieutenant?'

Franks scowled slightly.

'Yeah. It's all coming back to me now. This guy nearly cost me my pension. We found him outside the Tinklebell, that's a roadhouse five miles from town. He'd been dumped in somebody's car, in the luggage compartment. The guy who owned the car hadn't opened the compartment in days, so he couldn't help fix how long the dead man had been in there. It all wasted a lot of time fixing the approximate hour of death. You see, it was two in the morning when he was found, and the driver had been in the roadhouse five hours. We were able to establish that the body had been loaded on sometime during those hours, but it's a fairly wide time band.'

'I see what you mean. How was he killed?'

'That was a puzzler for a while, too. We couldn't see out there in the dark any apparent cause of death. It wasn't till we got him down to the morgue that we found out. The guy was fully dressed you see. What happened was, somebody put three bullets into him while he was naked, then put his clothes on afterwards. Two bullets were in his belly, the third, which was the first one fired, was smack in his heart. Chances are, the guy never knew what hit him. You can tell that, looking at the face.'

He was right about that, there was no suffering there, no pain.

'And these details about him, you got those from his pockets?'

'Yeah. There was no attempt to conceal his identity. And it wasn't because the killer didn't have time. Anybody who has time to dress a dead man has got time enough to empty his pockets.'

I helped myself to an Old Favorite. Like the lieutenant, I was beginning to feel we could be on to something here.

'From what you say, I get the impression there was no attempt to hide identity, because there wasn't any identity to hide. James Earnshaw began and ended at the Dunphy Apartments. No trails in, and none out.'

Franks inclined his head morosely.

'That was the way it stacked up at the time. This guy had an identity for just two days. The two days between the time we found him, and the time our report came through from L.A. That hair you see, that's a phoney too. A dye job, applied within hours before his death.'

Better and better. If Joe Judson came to Vale City, it could have been with the intention of changing his appearance, picking up whatever was owing to him, then starting over again as James Earnshaw.

'But he must have had some help,' I thought aloud.

'Huh? How was that?'

'Sorry, I was thinking aloud. I was thinking that somebody else helped him book that apartment. They don't usually accept advance rentals with a penitentiary return address. Or if they did, they'd certainly remember.'

'Correct. That is, assuming this guy is your man.'

'I'm getting more sure of it by the minute. By the way, what did you mean just now, when you said the case almost got you fired off the force?'

The ghost of a smile showed quickly on his face, and was as quickly dismissed.

'Almost funny now, thinking back. But nobody was laughing at the time. I hadn't been a lieutenant very long when this one broke. As

85

soon as I saw how he died, there at the morgue, I did some fast thinking. For a guy to be shot when he has no clothes on, he has to be inside some place. He also has to be with somebody, if you catch my drift. So here's a healthy looking man, with an out of town home address, murdered by somebody while he doesn't have any clothes on. That's point one. After he's dead, somebody gets him dressed and gets him out to the Tinklebell. That means at least two people. That's point two. They weren't ordinary people. Not because ordinary people don't commit murder, they do. But they don't have kindly neighbors who are going to help them dispose of the body. That's point three. So they're gang people, some kind of hoods. At least the ones helping with the body are. You can imagine the way I organized my thinking on that?'

'I think so. He was with some woman when it happened. It may have been planned or it may have just developed. But whether she killed him, or somebody she was working for did it, she was able to get help getting rid of him.'

Franks spread his shoulders helplessly.

'Natch. What else could I think? What would anybody think?'

'Pretty much the same, I imagine.'

'You should have tried convincing the commissioner. Brother, that was an interview

I'd like to forget.'

He sat there, thinking back to it.

'But I still don't know where you went wrong,' I reminded.

'Eh? Oh, yeah. I'll tell you. I called in every man, every car I could muster, and we jumped every cathouse in town. What a night. I got two councilmen, the owner of the biggest store in Vale, and the mayor's nephew.'

I chuckled at the mournful way he recited the story. He glared across, then began to chuckle to himself.

'Oh, it all sounds very funny now. But believe me, if I could've crawled into some hole in the ground at the time, that would have been fine with me. So what d'you think?'

He pointed at the white-haired Mr. James Earnshaw.

'I think we could be heading in the right direction,' I told him. 'I think Mr. Earnshaw might pay off. Is there any chance of a copy of this picture?'

'Sure, I'll arrange that.' He leaned forward and looked at me seriously. 'Look, I'm sure you know your own business, and they tell me you're good, but you're not seriously going to try cracking this, are you? I mean, there weren't any leads two years ago, and whatever we couldn't dig up then, you don't imagine you're going to find after all this time?'

There was just a suspicion of affronted professionalism behind the enquiry. I would have to answer carefully.

'No, I doubt if there's much hope of that. But I have a starting point which you didn't have. I shall be aiming to find out whether Earnshaw was Judson, not who killed him. And remember, I am not really interested in Judson at all. I'm really concerned with the people who knew him, and this may be a help.'

He seemed somewhat mollified as he sat back in the chair.

'Yeah, I see. H'm. Still, if you happen across any information which might help a plodding law officer to solve an old murder case, you'll have me in mind?'

I seemed to recall a similar interview with Ben Fawcett of the Fourth Precinct back home.

'You bet I will. Believe me, with all this cooperation I've had around here, anything I get is yours.'

I asked him the Los Angeles address again and wrote it down. Then I waited while the people outside took a copy of the picture for me.

'How about this Tinklebell?' I asked. 'What kind of place is that?'

He tutted.

'You don't know it? Best place in town. And coming from a policeman that means a lot. Good music, good food, best liquor for miles. You know, with places like that, you usually get mob guys moving in. Not out there.

There's no funny stuff, no gals, no green tables in back. Why, I don't believe we ever had so much as a drunk driver coming out of there. Do yourself a favor. Next time you want to date a girl to a real nice time, just head straight out to the Tinklebell. Tell Maggie I sent you. You'll have to pay just the same, but she might see you get a good table.'

'Maggie?' I queried.

'Sure. Maggie Murphy. She runs the place. But strict. A real one hundred per center.'

'I'll remember.'

Just then the copy of the Earnshaw picture was brought back. I thought I'd taken up enough of Franks' valuable time. And it looked as though it might not be wasted. I thanked him again, gathered up my few papers and left.

If I kept the pedal down, I'd be there in time for a late lunch in Los Angeles.

CHAPTER SEVEN

By heading north out of Vale I could pick up Highway Sixty six and then it was a straight road into L.A. Five miles along the road, I came across a huge board telling me that the Tinklebell was on my right hand side and just half a mile along. As I was so near, I decided I could spare ten minutes to take a quick look at a place which got such a glowing write-up from the police department.

I turned into the forecourt which was well laid out with neat flower-beds. An elderly man knelt beside one, pruning away with precision. I parked beside a brand new Toyota and went up the ranch-house steps into the iron-grilled entrance. On the left were two doors. The nearest one was marked 'Hombres'. I didn't need to look at the other. The door facing me was private, according to the gold lettering on it. That left just two doors on the right, one marked 'Grill Room' and the other 'Maggie's place'. I wasn't in need of any grill, so I elected for Maggie. It was a big room, forty feet long by about twenty, but the length was cunningly broken up by small alcoves and nooks. In the far corner, a gold grand piano looked faintly unhappy against the strong sunlight. There weren't many people around, maybe ten or a dozen scattered thinly. The bartender dusted at the rows of bottles.

'Morning,' I greeted.

He turned around quickly, putting down the yellow rag.

'Oh, say I'm sorry, I didn't see you come in. What'll you have?'

'Scotch over ice. Plenty of ice.'

He got busy on it. I hadn't named any brand, but he pulled out a bottle of Uncle Jock just the same. This guy was for me.

'You couldn't be Maggie?' I asked.

He grinned as he set down the cool glass.

'Oh, you mean the sign? No, I'm just the hired help. Maggie is Miss Murphy, she owns the place.'

'Is she around?'

He looked at me quickly, wondering who I was.

'No. She had to go out for a while. Can I give her a message?'

'Nothing special. I promised a friend of mine I'd look in if I came this way.'

'I see. A friend, you say?'

He didn't ask the name, but he wanted to know just the same.

'Lieutenant Franks, Vale City Police Department. The build-up he gave the place, a guy just has to come and see.'

The barman grinned, mopping delicately at a drop of water which slithered down the side of an ice-bucket.

'Oh, Mr. Franks, sure. He gets out here sometimes, Mrs. Franks too. Real nice people. Shall I tell Miss Murphy you dropped by?'

'Please. Preston is the name. I'm from Monkton City.'

He produced an inch of pencil and wrote the name down on a small pad.

'Sure, Mr. Preston, I'll tell her. Monkton eh? Nice city, real nice. I like to get over there when I can, take the kids. That's some swell beach you have there.'

'Yes,' I agreed. 'Still, you have a nice

91

surroundings here. A pleasant place to work, I imagine. You been here very long?'

'I'm the oldest inhabitant,' he announced proudly. 'Nearly five years now. And if you knew this business, believe me, five years almost qualifies a man for a pension.'

That was true enough. Bartenders have the itchiest feet of any occupation I know.

'That is a long time,' I nodded. 'Good spot here, eh?'

'The best,' he said enthusiastically. 'Most of the others have been here two or three years as well. I been in this business all my life, had some good bosses, and plenty of the other kind. But Miss Murphy, man, she is the most.'

I began to feel sorry I wasn't going to see the fabulous Maggie.

'Say,' I remembered, or seemed to, 'wasn't this the place you had the murder one time? Bout a year ago, or it may have been more.'

He moved closer towards me, lowering his voice.

'Look, Mr. Preston, no offense you understand, but if you must talk about that, could you be a little quieter?'

He inclined his head to the room at large, but nobody seemed to be paying us any attention.

'Oh,' and I dropped off a few decibels too, 'sorry. I don't suppose you want everybody reminded all the time.'

'We can live without it,' he admitted.

'Anyway, it was a long time ago.'

'Still,' I pressed, like any other excited member of the public. 'It must have been terrible. I mean, all those policemen and reporters and everything. Did you see the body yourself?'

'No,' he said, in that tone of voice that indicated he'd face it like a man if the ceiling happened to fall on my head. 'I was working in here. As for all those people, all I can tell you about them, especially the reporters, it was a good night for business around here. I never saw the place so busy at four in the morning. You'd have thought it was New Year's.'

This guy had nothing to tell me. And even if he had, I wasn't going to get it. You get into the habit of knowing these things, or else spend your life chasing up blind alleys.

'Oh.' I was disappointed. 'You don't really know much about it then?'

He shook his head in dismissal.

'Just what I read in the newspapers.'

There wasn't any point in my hanging around. I promised myself a look at Maggie Murphy some time, but it wouldn't be today.

'Well, nice talking to you. And that was a fine drink.' I left him enough of a tip so he'd remember he liked me if I ever went back.

Outside the old man was still at the same flower bed. It didn't look to me as though he'd moved. But there was no doubt that orderliness didn't get there all by itself. I

93

swung the Chev around and headed out for Highway Sixty-six.

There was plenty of traffic today, and I joined the steady stream on the great concrete ribbon, maintaining an even sixty all the way. At one-thirty I hit the outskirts of the big town, and was soon nosing along Hamilton Street, looking for a place to park. I was lucky, because some people had vacated spaces so they could drive to lunch. I found a spot just a block away from the Dunphy Apartments, and climbed thankfully out of the car. Any thoughts I may have had about eating had been burnt out of me during the ride. Instead, I headed for the apartment building, a huge oblong box which disappeared above me almost out of sight. The street level was the usual compact layout of stores and restaurants. I read a story one time about a guy lived in one of these places. Everything in the world anybody could want was right there inside the building. He could eat, drink, take a swim. He could buy groceries, clothes, get a shoe-shine or a haircut. There was even a movie theater and a residents club.

This man in the story was some kind of writer, so he didn't even have to leave the place to go to work. Gradually, he gave up trips outside until finally he became afraid to leave the protective nest anyway. He became afraid of simple things like traffic and strangers. In the end he went crazy and drowned himself in the heated swimming pool. The coroner passed a verdict of suicide while the balance of the mind was disturbed. The coroner also said there could be no other explanation, here was a man who had everything in the world anybody could possibly want. It was a creepy kind of story, and now, looking up at the smooth concrete face. I felt an anticipatory shiver.

I asked a cute little trick in a cigaret kiosk where I could locate the management, and she directed me to an office at the rear. I went along and opened the outer glass door. A girl sat behind the desk hardly big enough to support the shiny red typewriter she was picking at.

'Good afternoon,' she said mechanically. 'What can I do for you?'

She wasn't very old, eighteen or so, with a dull faded kind of complexion. To me, she seemed to be less of an individual person than an accessory part of the typewriter.

'I'd like to see the manager. About renting an apartment.'

'We don't have any vacancies,' she replied automatically. 'But if you care to leave your name and address, we will arrange to send you full details of any apartments which become available.'

'That's very good of you,' I said pleasantly, 'but I'd still like to have a few words with him.'

She looked affronted, the first human

reaction I'd seen so far. It was because I'd committed the error of not complying with the system.

'It won't do any good,' she told me crossly. 'But if you insist.'

She turned a knob on an inter-communicating panel beside the desk.

'Mr. Nelson, there's a man insists on seeing you about renting an apartment. Yes, I know. I already told him that.' She looked up at me with malevolent triumph. 'What name, please.'

'Preston. And tell him I've come all the way from Vale City just to see him for five minutes.'

She hesitated, then did as I asked. Then she said, pouting:

'You may go in, that door there. Mr. Nelson can only give you two minutes.'

I went through that door there, as a man was rising to greet me.

'Afternoon, Mr. Preston. I see you don't have an appointment, and I do have a very busy schedule.'

'Won't take much of your time, Mr. Nelson. I'm looking into the death of one of your tenants, and maybe you can help me.'

'Death?' he repeated blankly. 'But the girl said—'

'She said it was about renting an apartment. In a way it is. And it was a good enough story for her. I'm sure you would want to keep this talk restricted just to we two. You know how

96

quickly these things get spread around and distorted.'

'I see. Yes, yes, I quite see that. Very considerate of you. Now, this tenant, it's very unlikely I can help you. We have upwards of four thousand people living here. Most of them I never even laid eyes on.'

He said it with quiet pride. It was evidently a matter of some prestige that the man who ran the place should have as little contact as possible with the people he was running it for. I could see the future in his face. In fifty years, maybe twenty, the manager would never see any of the inmates—sorry—tenants, at all. If we really hustled up with progress, maybe he wouldn't even need to see the building either.

'Still, Mr. Nelson, I think you might just bring this one to mind. You see, this man was murdered.'

His face went white. Very slowly he took from an inside pocket a snowy white handkerchief and converted it to a dirty limp rag against his face.

'Murdered,' he repeated flatly. 'A murder here at Dunphy?'

'Oh no,' I corrected. 'He wasn't actually murdered here. It was over in Vale City. He just happened to be one of your tenants at the time.'

He glowered at me over the damp handkerchief.

'Mr. Preston, I am not a well man. You

don't have any business coming here saying things like that. Why I might have had a seizure. Which of the tenants is it?'

'Not is, was,' I amended. 'This happened two years ago. Man by the name of Earnshaw, James Earnshaw.' He was fully recovered now. Stowing the ex-handkerchief away, he said:

'How would I know what happened then? I wasn't even here.'

'Oh.'

I looked disappointed, and sounded it. It was no act.

'Who was manager before you?'

'There wasn't one. The holding company used to operate the apartments from their central office. Then they found the work was taking up too much of their time, and looked around for someone suitable.'

He tried not to smirk as he described himself.

'Congratulations. Where do I find this holding company?'

'Believe me, you'd only be wasting your time. They don't keep—'

His voice tailed away at my hostile stare.

'Do I understand you don't wish to cooperate in a case of homicide? Do I take it the Dunphy Apartments wish to obstruct justice? Boy, I just love to think what the yellow sheets will make of that.'

'Enough.' Nelson waved a flabby hand. 'I really can't stand any more of this. Dunphy

98

Realty Co. corner of Hudson and Tenth.'

'Thanks.'

I went out. The sullen girl stared at me emptily.

'Better watch out for your boss,' I suggested. 'He probably won't last out the day in this heat.'

Hudson and Tenth was across town, and I did my share of fuming and horn-blowing before I reached there. The company was situated on fourteen, naturally. I went up in the express elevator, surprised as ever to find myself emerging before I realized we'd started. The Dunphy Realty Co. was one of a whole list of companies on the sandalwood indicator outside the soundproof glass doors. Inside was a fair hubbub of busy people. I leaned on the leather surface where it said 'Enquiries' and leered at a dark number who was not without her points.

She asked what I wanted, and we kidded that around for a while. When I started making sense she lost interest and switched me to an office the size of a broom cupboard. A fair eager young man got up, or rather bounced up. His name was Penny, and he was glad, yes glad, to do whatever he could. Whatever he could did not include anything very specific about the Dunphy Apartments. No, he didn't know of the case himself. No, he hadn't been with the company two years earlier. No, they didn't retain records more than twelve months after a tenant departed. Yes he'd be glad to check it. He checked it.

'I'm extremely sorry, Mr. Preston, but you can understand the company wouldn't have a need to keep old papers of that kind. Even in the—um—rather unusual circumstances.'

Yes, I could understand. And yes, if anything occurred to me where the company, and in particular Mr. Penny, could be of help, I'd most certainly call him. Almost before I knew it, I was back standing on the hot pavement outside the building, wondering what kind of crazy impulse had driven me here anyway. Still, as I was in Los Angeles, I may as well get the full benefit of my visit.

What I needed right then was a telephone. And not just any old telephone, but a special kind. The kind that comes with or without a private booth, but is situated on an inside wall. The inside wall, in turn, is not more than eight feet away from a long mahogany bar behind which a kindly man dispenses cold beer to people who are waiting to use the telephone. One of the many civilized attractions of L.A. is that there are many such telephones available. I am not exactly a stranger to the city, and I knew of a place within a few minutes walk with exactly the required type of phoning facilities. Soon I was burying my nose in zero temperature foam, while the icy liquid poured smoothly down a grateful throat.

'You look like you needed that,' chuckled the bar jockey.

'Great invention, the telephone,' I said solemnly.

He looked at me twice, decided I was one of those customers, and found something to do at the other end of the bar. I picked up the beer, and went to the small pile of directories by the telephone. It seemed to me, so long as I was in the city, that I might as well look up Elmo Davis. He was the lawyer who handled the sale of the Four Horsemen, when Dee bought it two years ago. The name of the company he represented then was A.B. Amusements, and he probably knew no more about this whole thing than a certain bartender who was at that point in time anxiously watching to see I didn't rip the phone out of the wall. He should worry. The directory was more than five years old. One thing about a name like Davis, you can always be certain you're going to have no trouble finding it. The difficulty arises when it comes to locating a particular Davis. In the directory I was thumbing over, I could have a whole flock of Davis's, four complete pages of them. There wasn't any Elmo listed, but there were three Davis E's who had some kind of legal connections. The first one I got denied that his name was Elmo. This got me excited, a clear case of identity suppression. It finally emerged the man's name was Egbert, and I made sounds of sympathy before breaking the connection. Second time out, I struck.

'Would you be a Mr. Elmo Davis?' I queried.

'Yes. What can I do for you?'

I did two quick dance steps, caught the bartender's eye and froze.

'Like to see you Mr. Davis. I'm only in Los Angeles for an hour. This wouldn't take more than five minutes.'

He fretted about being busy and so forth, finally agreed to give me five minutes if I went to his office immediately. I put down the phone, carried my beer back to the counter, and stood in front of the watchful man on the other side.

'Alexander Graham Bell,' I toasted, tipping the remaining beer down. I think if I'd stayed another minute, he'd have called the police.

CHAPTER EIGHT

Lawyers come in all shapes and sizes, like anybody else. To listen to some people, you'd imagine a man just had to be a lawyer, and he was one step away from Supreme Court Justice. In fact, that is far from the truth. There are good ones and bad ones, successful ones and failures. The successful are not always good, and the failures are not all bad.

There are one-man firms, multiples, partnerships. There are also lawyer criminals, but due to their training, we don't get to hear so much about that variety.

Elmo Davis seemed to have made it big. He handled the business of a whole flock of companies, and he needed two floors of a tall building to do it in. I tried the lower floor first, and they sent me tramping up three flights of stairs to try again. The counter was black glass, with a gold ink stand resting on it. There was no ink.

'Did you wish to borrow a pen?'

The voice was cool, very cool. I looked at the girl it belonged to, and she was very cool, too. Glacial in fact, with a pale made up face and skimpy blonde hair. Just to add a dash of colour to the ensemble she wore a crisp white shirt-blouse and a dark gray skirt. She must know a lot about the law, I decided. There'd be no other excuse for her being employed outside a horror movie.

'No. I want to see Mr. Davis. The name is Preston.'

The eyes, too, were like chipped ice.

'Sorry, Mr. Davis is tied up. If you would care to write in for an appointment?'

She pulled out a glass tray on a slide, and looked at a typed list.

'There's no Preston here. Mr. Davis always insists—'

'Lady,' I interrupted gently. 'It's great

talking with you and everything, but I don't have all day to waste. I arranged an appointment with him over the telephone not twenty minutes ago. Now will you either take me to him, or go and get someone who can do something?'

She pushed the tray in hard enough to make me fear for the glass surface.

'Wait,' she snapped.

I waited while she disappeared through a blond oak door. A minute later she was back, raising a grooved flap at the end of the counter.

'Mr. Davis' personal secretary will see you.'

And from the way she spoke, there was no doubt Mr. Davis' personal secretary would know exactly how to handle my kind. I went meekly behind her down a carpeted corridor to the end room. Here she knocked and waited till she was invited in.

'This is the man I told you about, Miss Peters.'

She didn't offer to move out of the way, so I had to brush past her into the room. The first thing I saw was the girl standing by the window. She was also the second thing I saw, and well worth the seeing.

She stood, looking at me with amused appraising eyes, while I took in one or two points. Like for instance, she was tallish maybe five seven, slender without being skinny. Her hair was the color of burnished copper and fell in deep waves around the oval face. She had green eyes naturally, and a good nose, not one of these button jobs. The lips were warm and full, slightly parted now over the gleaming teeth as she watched me.

'Don't you usually say anything?' she mocked.

'There's a time for talking and a time for looking,' I replied. 'I don't feel like talking for a while.'

She chuckled, a low musical sound.

'If you think this'll help you get in to Mr. Davis, you're mistaken. It's been tried before.'

I shook my head. The neat linen suit was lime green, or maybe a shade darker. Cut on strictly business lines, it didn't do one solitary thing to hide the full splendid body inside.

'Honey, this is entirely on my own time. I don't need any help to see Mr. Davis. I have an appointment.'

'Not according to me,' she contradicted. 'And I would know.'

I looked around at the office, finally. I was wondering how much it cost to date a girl who had her own panelled office and a crimson carpet a man could lose his shoes in.

'He didn't tell you? Wasn't more than twenty minutes ago. I called him on the 'phone.'

The copper hair waved a little as she shook her head.

'No. All the calls come through me. See?'

She pointed at the three phones on her desk. One of them had a box underneath with several switches. With the girl outside, I could get mad, never with the delectable Miss Peters.

'Look Miss Peters, I realize you have to protect him, but couldn't he just have easily have said no, he wouldn't see me? Ask him.'

She hesitated, no longer quite so positive.

'I'll play too, if you insist. What number did you call?'

'Er—er—'

I couldn't remember, but luckily I'd scribbled it down. Fishing the paper from my pocket, I read the number to her. Now, she looked surprised.

'But that's his classified number,' she objected. 'How did you get hold of it?'

'It wasn't easy,' I admitted. 'I had to thumb through a directory in a local bar. Must have taken all of two minutes.'

Understanding came into her eyes, and what had been the beginnings of suspicion disappeared.

'Ah, one of those. Yes, it does happen sometimes. It must have been very old. That number hasn't been listed in years. Well, you seem to have achieved the impossible, Mr. Preston.'

'I wouldn't have got this far if that—er— other young lady had her way.'

Again she chuckled, and I decided I liked being around Miss Peters.

'Did she give you a bad time? You mustn't blame her too much. That's one of the reasons she's employed here.'

'Oh I don't,' I said magnanimously. 'I guess she's found things tough since they stopped making all those Boris Karloff pictures.'

She bent her head to flick down one of the keys of below the middle telephone, so I couldn't see whether she smiled or not.

'I have a Mr. Preston out here, Mr. Davis. He apparently spoke to you on the private phone? Yes, right away.'

She walked across the room with an easy graceful stride, making a face so I'd follow. She needn't have bothered, I'd have followed her anyway. As she made to open a door in the far wall, I put a hand on her arm.

'Just a minute. Do I come out this way too?'

'Why?'

But she didn't shrug off the hand.

'Because I want to talk to you again,' I said honestly. The green eyes looked at me thoughtfully.

'Come out this way. Tell him you left something in here.'

Then she opened the door, and I went into Elmo Davis' office. I don't say it's the biggest place in the world. I've seen bigger. Like the Rose Bowl, Yankee Stadium, and one or two other spots. It seemed to stretch in all directions. Way off in the distance a man sat behind a desk the size of a Sherman tank.

That's the desk, not the man. I began the long trek across acres of carpet, almost tempted to run in case some helmeted thug brought me down before I made the fifteen yard line.

'Mr. Preston?'

Davis was a small man. It wasn't till I got closer I realized he was standing, and that made him even smaller than my first impression. A wizened, lined face inspected me through gold nose-glasses. He didn't offer to shake hands.

'Mr. Preston,' he repeated, 'I am a very busy man. Tell me one thing, how did you learn my private number?'

I went through my routine about the bar again.

'I see,' he nodded. 'Would you be good enough to tell me the name of this—um—bar?'

I began to speak, then stopped as a thought came into my head.

'I will, with pleasure,' I assured him, 'but first, how about you telling me something, Mr. Davis?'

He looked affronted. You don't get an office the size of Radio City by having people talk back to you.

'Well?' he barked squeakily.

'Mr. Davis, the only reason you agreed to see me was so you could find out where I got your telephone number. Right?'

'Right. I don't know any Preston. I do not

intend to know any Preston. But it was worth two minutes of my time to learn how you obtained that number. The address please, then you may leave.'

The nerve of the man was impressive. He said all this without cracking a grin. Such was the might of Elmo Davis, I was permitted to assume, that there was no question of whether I might want to leave. This Davis had been pushing people around for too long, and I didn't need anything from him, except information. Shaking my head sadly, I stretched out in a chair close by the desk.

'Mr. Davis,' I told him, 'you ought to run a bus line through here. You're losing touch with the common people. I will leave after I get what I came for. Otherwise I will personally go out and write your private number on every hoarding in the city.'

'Don't be childish,' he fretted. 'What would that profit you?'

'Nothing,' I conceded. 'But I'm kind of a persistent person. You have some information right at your fingertips and I need it. And as for being childish Mr. Davis, we make a fine-looking pair.'

He tutted and clicked his teeth. Then abruptly, he sat down.

'What is it you want?' he snapped. 'Mind you, if it involves anything confidential to a client, you are wasting your time.'

'That's fair enough. About two years ago,

109

you acted as intermediary in the sale of a property on Pioneer Street, Monkton City. The people you represented were A.B. Amusements. The man who bought the place was named Dee. Do you remember?'

He uttered a high, brittle snort.

'Remember? Why should I possibly remember? I am not a small-town one clerk operation. I never handle these things personally. My people,' he waved a hand around, 'they probably deal with fifty such transactions a month. Even the man who carried out the work is unlikely to recall it, much less myself.'

'Quit being so important all the time,' I suggested. 'I guess this organization keeps files doesn't it?'

Irritably he barked:

'Miss Peters, I want the file on a sale by A.B. Amusements of a place on Pioneer Street, Monkton City. Purchaser, Dee. Date about two years ago.' Then looking at me: 'What was the number of the property?'

'It's 925. And the place is called the Four Horsemen.'

'You heard that, Miss Peters. The Four Horsemen. And I am in something of a hurry.'

We sat out the full minute. Davis wasn't going to fill up the time with social chit chat. He stared past out across the dim horizon towards the far end of the room. I stared at a picture on the opposite wall which appeared to represent a man's head. At least some parts of it did. I mean that thing on the right there was certainly an ear, no doubt of it. And up on top, that was hair, surely? At least, one part of it was hair. The other was an assortment of yellow and black squares and circles. There was an eye, too, only it seemed to be growing on a stalk at the side of the head where the other ear should be. I didn't like the picture. I liked the sense of humor of the guy who produced it though. He had to be a man I could get along with. Somebody who could use up a few cents' worth of paint and about an hour of nightmare activity, and then persuade somebody who could pay the kind of money an Elmo Davis could pay, that this was something for his office wall. Yes I could get along with a man like that. The door opened and the delectable Miss Peters came in. I could get along with her too, given the opportunity. Davis didn't even look at her as she walked up to the desk, but I was doing enough looking for both of us.

She rested a file in front of him. He didn't thank her, merely started turning over papers. Turning, she looked quickly at me, face a little puzzled, then carried out her exit performance.

'Very well,' Davis' high-pitched voice cut across my pleasant thoughts. 'It appears you may be correct. We did handle this transaction. What of it?'

'I'm interested in A.B. Amusements,' I told him.

'Then you had better approach them, not me.'

'I'll be glad to,' I assured him. 'If you'll just tell me exactly who they are.'

'My clients' affairs are not for discussion with anyone who chances to walk in from the street,' he said loftily.

'I don't want to discuss their affairs,' I returned. 'I just want to know who they are. What reason can you have for concealing their identity, Mr. Davis? Unless there's perhaps some illegal involvement?'

'Illegal—? Poppycock. How dare you make such an insinuation?'

'I don't insinuate anything. But I have reason, good reason, to think these people are criminals, Mr. Davis. People the police would like a chance to talk with. Of course, if you are refusing to cooperate, I have no doubt a subpoena could be issued. I was hoping you wouldn't want that kind of thing associated with your firm.'

'Police?' he muttered. 'Subpoena. Just who or what are you? If you are a police officer you had only to say so.'

'Correct. And I'm not a police officer. This is who I am.'

I took out my sticker and handed it across to him. He looked at it, pursed his lips and handed it back.

'What kind of police involvement?' he queried. 'Not that it will damage me in the slightest.'

'No, it probably won't,' I admitted. 'But it would be preferable from your point of view if you weren't associated with the matter at all. If I can locate these A.B. Amusements people, I need never mention how I found them. That way, nobody will ever know that file is lying in your system. Everybody will be satisfied.'

'I asked you what kind of involvement,' he repeated.

'Well now, a nice mixed bag. There's pornography, one or two other small matters like that. Then there's murder, Mr. Davis.'

'Murder?'

'Yes. A man was murdered. I think these people may know something of it, if we can put faces on them.'

'I see. And you assure me I shall hear no more of it once I've given the names?'

'No,' I said frankly, 'I couldn't guarantee it. Not positively. I will guarantee that I'll keep you out of it, but I can't honestly say just how far the police will dig once they start.'

'Good,' he said, to my surprise. 'If you'd not said that, I'd have put the file away. You gave what sounds like an honest undertaking. And I'm prepared to meet you on those terms.'

Life, as they say, is full of surprises.

'Here we are, do you have a pencil? The company was owned by two people. Mr. and

Mrs. James Earnshaw.'

The pencil stopped of its own accord. Davis blinked at me.

'Something wrong?'

'No,' I said quickly. 'Was there an address?'

'Yes, I have it here. Oh, that's odd.'

'What's odd?'

'Er—nothing,' and the set of his lips told me the subject was closed. 'The address is, or was at that time, 2727 Dunphy Apartments.'

James Eamshaw, 2727 Dunphy Apartments. It was like a recurring dream. Only now we had a Mrs. James Earnshaw too. And that was a girl I wanted to talk to very much indeed.

Davis sat staring at the papers in front of him. I was busy with my own thoughts, and started when he suddenly said:

'Murder, I think you said?'

'That's right, Mr. Davis. As you've been so helpful, I'll tell you a little more. The murdered man was one James Earnshaw, at the address you just gave me.'

He looked at me narrowly, dropping his head back to peer through the nose glasses.

'Are you telling me in your curious way, that you've been wasting my time young man?'

'No sir,' I assured him warmly. 'Your time has been well spent. It's my time that's been wasted. You see, I was hoping your information might give me a lead to people who could help me trace whoever killed James Eamshaw. I seem to have come full circle, and

114

that means I have to start all over. However, that's hardly your fault. I certainly appreciate—'

'Sit down.'

I'd been in the process of getting to my feet, but when Elmo Davis said sit down, people sat. I sat.

'Tell me about this Earnshaw,' he invited. 'Why should anybody want to kill him? Was he a rich man?'

'I don't know,' I confessed. 'Of course there'd be whatever money changed hands on the sale of the Four Horsemen. I don't know how much that was.'

And he didn't offer to tell me either.

'And Mrs. Earnshaw? What do you know of her?' he pressed.

'I didn't know there was any Mrs. Earnshaw until you told me,' I admitted. 'That's the one I have to find now.'

'You may be in luck,' he said gleefully, rubbing his hands. If appearances were anything to go by, Elmo Davis was excited. 'You have aroused my curiosity, Mr. Preston, damned if you haven't. You know why?'

'No, sir.'

'I probably look and act to you like an important big-city lawyer. That would be a correct impression, because that is precisely what I am. But you're not so naïve as to imagine they handed me all this when I graduated from law school?'

'No. I imagine there was a little work put in,

115

between times.'

'Hah.'

It was a brief explosive sound, and with it he jumped up from his chair and walked around the desk.

'A little work, you said? Hah. I worked ten and twelve hours a day for twenty years before I finally began to make any real impression. However, there is nothing so sickening as listening to an old man yapping about his success story.'

He could have fooled me. I would have sworn he was all set for a blow by blow description of his early struggles. He didn't appear to be expecting any comment, so I kept quiet.

'No, what I was going to tell you was this. For one period, in those early days, I acted for a firm of private investigators. People like you. In those three, or was it four years, I learned more about the law, more about people than in any other period. I still draw today on experiences I had back then. Except, of course, I no longer get the excitement. You follow me?'

'Mr. Davis,' I began slowly, 'I don't believe there's anything in all this that would interest you.'

'Rubbish. And don't be so independent. People can always use a smart lawyer. And I am a very smart lawyer, Mr. Preston. On top of which, I have certain information, which you do not.'

And if I wanted it, I had to humor him.

'Well, naturally, only a fool ever turns away help.'

'Good. I might be able to help, at that.' Leaning back over the desk he said, 'Miss Peters, I want to see Harvey Robbins, at once.'

That said, he came up straight again, and patted me on the shoulder. It was quite a switch from our first relationship.

'You were right not to turn me down,' he approved. 'Let's just see what we can make of all this. Mind, I promise nothing. But at the very least it might save you following up useless enquiries.'

That made sense too. I got back to studying the picture again, and I didn't like it any better the second time. There came a double tap at the other door, the non-Peters door.

'Come in.'

It opened, and in came a man of thirty-five or so, florid and heavy fleshed. He didn't look at me at all, eyes all for the bird-like figure behind the big desk.

'Ah Harvey. This is Mr. Preston. I am helping him over a few matters.' He saw me now, and extended a warm firm hand to this welcome visitor who was being helped by Elmo Davis.

'Glad to know you,' he enthused.

I mumbled some thing equally foolish, and sat again. 'Now Harvey, you remember the

Four Horsemen transaction?'

Davis said it in a tone of confident assumption, and waited for his subordinate's reaction. Harvey looked intelligently puzzled.

'The Four Horsemen, sir? Er let me see, that was er, was that the title of one of those novels where we secured the film rights for'— he looked at me and paused—'for a certain major studio?'

Davis smiled. A thin watery effort.

'No Harvey,' he tormented. 'It was not.'

'It has a very familiar ring sir. Perhaps if I just glanced at the file?'

But his boss made no move to pass over the file.

'The vendor was a man named Earnshaw. You recall Earnshaw? Two years ago?'

Robbins' face was now positively unhappy.

'Two years, you say sir? Well, it doesn't spring to mind right off hand. Earnshaw?'

'All right.' Davis gave it up in disgust. 'You fellers today, let me tell you, you don't know you're born. You have so much law business, business I bring here, you can't recall what you were doing two years back. Let me tell you, when I was your age, things were different. Business didn't hang down from the trees in those days. You'd have asked me what I was doing two years before, if I was doing anything at all, I could have told you the names of every one of the principal parties, and every condition in the agreement. Here.'

He slid the file over disgustedly. Harvey Robins made a little bobbing gesture with his head and turned quickly at the papers.

'Yes,' he muttered, 'this was one of mine.'

'We know that,' snapped Davis. 'That's why you're in here. Do you remember it?'

'It's a very straightforward transaction,' said Robins slowly. 'Payment was in full and in cash. The whole thing occupied only a few hours of office time. No sir, there's nothing here I'd need to remember.'

Davis clucked with irritation. Personally, I thought he was being unnecessarily tough with the unfortunate Harvey. And all because he wanted to play detective.

'Did you meet these people?' he persisted.

'Why yes. There's a note of a meeting right here in the office, when Mr. and Mrs. Earnshaw attended. That was the normal routine meeting, when I explained any odd points of law before they signed. I have no note of anything unusual.'

He looked at me for support, but I couldn't help him.

'Nobody said it was unusual,' said Davis tetchily. 'Do you remember these people?'

Harvey shrugged. He was a beaten man.

'No sir, I do not. People are in and out of my office every day of the week. I might recall somebody for a few days, a few weeks even. But two years? No sir, I'm afraid that's beyond me.'

He looked so woebegone, I thought I'd get him off the hook.

'That meeting in your office, Mr. Robbins, do you have the date?'

Now he could get something right, make a contribution.

'Certainly, Mr. Preston. Right here. It was March 26.'

I wrote it down, not because I'd forget it, but so Robbins would know I found it useful. He looked at me gratefully.

'All right, Harvey,' his boss said, 'we'll leave that subject.'

'Yes sir, Mr. Davis. Thank you. Will you be needing me for anything else?'

He was all set to make a bolt for the door, but Davis had other ideas.

'Yes, I will,' and the old man looked at me triumphantly. 'Don't I seem to recall that you handle the business for the Dunphy Realty Company?'

I sat up straight then. Maybe all this wasn't going to turn out such a bust after all. Harvey adjusted himself to the new topic.

'Why er, yes. Yes sir. That is, my staff look after it.'

'You'll have noticed from the file that the Earnshaws gave their address as being the Dunphy Apartments?'

'Yes, I saw that. It didn't strike me as particularly—'

'And now think about this. Mr. Earnshaw, of

the Dunphy Apartments, was murdered. When did you say that was, Mr. Preston?'

'Two years ago. April 18,' I contributed. Comprehension came on to Robbins' heavy features.

'I see. Just a few weeks after this transaction was completed.'

'Just twenty-three days to be exact,' I muttered.

Davis coughed and looked at me, anxious that I should not take over the questioning. Well, it was his office.

'Did it not strike you at the time as an odd coincidence? Did you not even remember that you had dealings with the man only a few days before he was killed?'

Harvey looked blank.

'Mr. Davis, I probably would have registered some kind of reaction if I had known the man was murdered. In fact, I'm certain of it. But I don't recall that I ever knew it.'

'Really Harvey, you are not coming through at all well,' Davis was getting excited. 'You do read the newspapers, I imagine? You've heard we have a space program in this country? You know about the presidential elections every fourth year?'

Harvey Robins bit his lip, and I could see he'd had all he was going to take.

'Mr. Davis, I read three newspapers every day. Not one, but three. I am as well-informed as any man in this city.'

He might have gone on to say something he'd regret, but old man Davis didn't give him the opportunity.

'And yet people can go around butchering your clients, *my* clients, and it just passes you by?'

'Mr. Davis,' I cut in. 'Maybe I can help a little here. This man Earnshaw wasn't killed in Los Angeles. He was found over in Vale City. That's point one. Here in L.A. you have enough violence right in your own backyard to fill up the important news space. A little item from Vale City was very probably buried at the foot of page twelve. And point two is, this Earnshaw was unknown at the Dunphy Apartments, so there was no local color at all. Nobody knew him, nobody had ever seen him, so you see there was no angle to make it worth playing up in your papers here. In fact until I met Mr. Robbins, I'd never talked to anybody who ever saw Earnshaw in the flesh. Not while he was alive, that is.'

Davis snorted and steamed, but he could see the sense of what I was saying. While he was calming down, I asked Robbins:

'Tell me, if you saw a picture of this man, do you think there's any possibility you'd remember him?'

He shrugged helplessly.

'I'm sorry, Mr. Preston, like to help you if I could. But you can see my position? An hour's

122

conversation, two years ago.'

Unfortunately, I could see his position only too well.

'Sure,' I agreed despondently. 'It would hardly make for a first class unshakable identification, would it?'

He spread his hands apologetically. Ten minutes earlier, Harvey Robbins had probably been full of confidence and zing, but in that short time he had been reduced to the status of a man who knew nothing, remembered nothing. And all without justification.

'Don't feel too badly, Mr. Robbins,' I encouraged. 'I can never remember anything that happened a week ago. There is one thing you may be able to tell me.'

'If I can.'

'Did you have any other address from these people, the Earnshaws? I mean before or after the Dunphy Apartments?'

He pulled the file from under his arm and flicked over papers.

'Yes. There is a note here. Mrs. Earnshaw could be contacted at 925 Pioneer Street, Apartment C. But surely that's—?'

He turned further into the file.

'Yes, Mr. Robbins,' I said sadly, 'it is. That's the address of the Four Horsemen. There are a few apartments above. Still, no telling. It could be useful.'

He nodded, not convinced, and went out. Davis cackled.

'Of course, I'm not in touch with up-to-date methods, Mr. Preston, but back in my day I would have said this was a very neat job of track-covering. These Earnshaws seem to have moved in a very tight circle indeed.'

'Yeah,' I agreed glumly. 'And things are not much more advanced today than in your time, Mr. Davis. I don't have any magic way of getting round all this. To me it looks like stalemate.'

He looked at me shrewdly.

'Giving up? I wouldn't have thought you were the type.'

I got up, pulling my jacket smooth.

'My client gave me less than forty-eight hours to clear this particular jungle. I think I might have made some progress if I had a little more time. But time I don't have. At least, I have plenty of my own, but I'm not a one-man crusade against crime. When I'm getting paid, I work. Once the money stops, I seize up.'

'A very practical approach to your particular calling. Nonetheless, I'm glad you happened, Mr. Preston. You've quite enlivened my day.'

He offered his hand this time.

'If anything occurs to you, if there's any piece of information you think might help, don't hesitate to call me.' I nodded, busily writing on a scrap of paper.

'Thanks. And here's the name of that bar.'

I went to the door leading to Miss Peters' office, waved and went out. She was sitting this

124

time, sideways to the desk, with the long splendid legs neatly crossed.

'You must have made quite an impression in there,' she told me. 'I expected you out under a minute.'

'Could you hear it all?' I wondered.

'No. Why do you ask?'

'I noticed that when he wanted you, he just called. He didn't press any switches or anything. Not that I could see.'

'Oh, that. No, it's a special gadget of his. Some kind of low-powered directional microphone. It only operates when he points his voice directly at it. Cost a small fortune.'

'I can imagine. Well, Miss Peters, my reason for being *here* is quite simple. How about having dinner with me tonight?'

She inspected me in a way that made me wonder whether my suit was crumpled.

'Why?'

'Because you have to eat anyway, so do I. Because you have a kind face, and you might be the type to take pity on a poor stranger in a great big city.'

'You're wrong there. I don't have time nor inclination to look after the lame dogs of this world, Mr. Preston. I'm all through with that. But, since you are undoubtedly the phoniest lame dog I've met this week, I'll come.'

'Fine.'

I arranged to meet her at seven, outside a place called the Dust Bowl, then left. Outside I got another helping of the frozen treatment from the Dracula's daughter character. I grinned at her pleasantly, wondering what she'd say if she knew who was having dinner with me.

Downstairs, in front of the building, I saw Harvey Robbins climbing into a cab, his red face even redder in the late afternoon sun. It had not been a good day for Mr. Robbins. Still, some of us had made all kinds of progress. Maybe I wasn't doing too well in the search for Anthea Horan, but I certainly had a big consolation prize by way of Miss Peters.

It occurred to me I hadn't even asked her first name.

CHAPTER NINE

'It's Louise.'

'Mine's Mark. Here's to you, Louise.'

She looked at me seriously. She seemed to be a more serious girl than outward appearances would indicate.

Every now and then I would find her looking at me like that.

'Martini all right?'

'It's fine, thank you. They always do a good martini here. Tell me about yourself, Mark.'

'Like what about me? I've been around a long time. Could be a very long story.'

'I'm in no hurry,' she assured me. 'What do you do? What kind of a job is it that gets you in to see Mr. Davis, and then permits you to stay all that time?'

I hesitated. This was a girl I liked. This was also a girl who worked for a very powerful L.A. lawyer, a girl who knew what time of day it was. I liked to think she was with me because she liked my big blue eyes. That was what I liked to think. But I don't have big blue eyes. I liked to think she was with me because of my irresistible charm, but I seemed to recall that some women had found resistance possible. And I mustn't hesitate too long.

'I'm trying to locate someone,' I told her. 'I thought Mr. Davis might be able to help.'

'You didn't answer me,' she pointed out.

'Yes I did. I find people.'

'Well,' she said slowly, 'you're not from the Bureau of Missing Persons. If you were, you wouldn't have wasted all that time in my office.'

'I didn't consider it wasted,' I demurred.

'Now, don't interrupt,' she reprimanded. 'Let's see, we've crossed off the F.B.I. That leaves er—insurance?'

'Sometimes,' I admitted.

'Good, I'm warmer. Just a moment.'

She closed her eyes and concentrated. To do this she had to frown lightly, and on her it looked good. After a few moments she opened her eyes and gave me one of her slow appraisals.

'You're a private detective,' she announced.

'Do you mind?'

'I don't know. I'll have to think about it, get to know you. Frankly, it isn't a very good beginning. I've met a few in the course of my work, and overall I can't say I've been impressed.'

'Every trade has its bums,' I protested. 'Oh, I know the guys you mean. Always looking for the percentage, and not too particular where it comes from. There are a few of those. All right, there are too many of those. This business is regrettably wide open for the blackmail artist, the fast shuffler, the sticky finger brigade. But we're not all like that. Look at me.'

'I am looking at you. And I'm thinking I want to believe you. I don't often feel that way about a person. When I do, I'm not usually wrong.'

She had a very direct way of speaking, which was disconcerting at first, but which I rapidly came to appreciate.

'Tell me about Mr. Davis,' she went on. 'Was he able to help you? Or perhaps I should say, was he willing?'

I sipped at the frosted martini, nodding.

'He was not only able and willing, he was ready. Yeah, he helped me quite a little. Not in a very positive sense, but in the negative way that he was able to close a few doors I needn't bother to open again. In my business that's valuable. Ninety per cent of my enquiries are stillborn. If I can get warned off certain angles, it saves time. My time is money.'

'But not your money?' she asked. 'You're usually working for someone else, aren't you?'

'Yes,' I explained patiently. 'But people hire me to get things done. They don't want me coming around for my pension on their time. Besides, it's a matter of professional pride.'

I went all professionally proud. Louise chuckled.

'I begin to think perhaps you really are a little different from some of the people we've had through the office. Some of them are quite unprofessional and not in the least proud. Are you good at it?'

'Being proud?'

I misunderstood her deliberately to see if I could disturb her calm.

'No, at being a private detective.'

'Not bad. Not bad at all. My license is reviewed annually you know by the State Commission, and it's been renewed more years than I'm going to admit to you. I have a fairly large apartment, the bank manager speaks to me. Anything else?'

To my astonishment, she sang in a low sweet voice:

'He was setting out his stall
For a wedding in the fall.'

129

Some people at a nearby table caught a snatch of the old melody and turned to look at us, grinning with approval. I felt myself turning red, but I laughed just the same.

'I guess it did sound a little that way,' I confessed. 'Why should I feel that I have to explain myself to you? I've only known you a few hours, and all we're doing is waiting for dinner.'

She gazed at me over the rim of the long-stemmed glass.

'Is it Mark? I wonder.'

This was crazy. This was little short of plain insanity. Here I was, busy telling this girl, this stranger, what a helluva guy I was, boasting like some kid on the high school team. This is Preston, remember? I can take dames, or leave 'em alone. Come to that, I can take them, and then leave them alone. What was getting into me, that this Louise Peters was putting there? Who did she think she was, letting the lights reflect from the burnished copper head that way? And she needn't have worn that black dress, caught up at the throat so the rich cream of her skin showed against the soft material like buttermilk. Not that there was any of the farm about this Peters. She was all big town, and she'd eaten plenty like me before, no doubt. That was what I was, I was just the next item on the menu. Well, we'd see about that. I wasn't exactly a stranger to this kind of situation myself.

'And what did you decide?'

The soft question cut suddenly into my thoughts.

'Huh, decide?'

'You were thinking about something, and you came to a decision,' she informed me. 'I could tell by your face.'

Thought reading, yet. Well a guy has to watch out for his defenses.

'Oh, I was miles away,' I dismissed.

'Is she pretty?'

There, you see? She wasn't right all the time.

'There isn't any she,' I told her. 'Not the way you mean.'

'Oh? And what way do I mean?'

I had her now. This was firm ground, the old chatter between a man and a woman, about what makes her so special.

'You mean somebody I'm involved with,' I explained. 'Like a fiancée, or a steady date, that kind of thing.'

'Or a wife,' she supplemented. 'That kind of thing too.'

'That too.'

She could sense the action was about to be unprofitable, so she switched the attack.

'I don't want to pry too much, but I wouldn't have thought a city the size of Vale would produce enough of your kind of work to keep you busy all year round.'

'Vale?'

'Yes. That was where you said you came from, this afternoon.'

She withdrew slightly, as though afraid she was about to catch me out in a lie.

'Oh, that,' I remembered. 'No, I said I'd come direct from Vale City to L.A. It's not my town, I was there looking for someone. Same someone I came to ask Mr. Davis about. My home town is Monkton City. You know it?'

'I've been there a couple of times.'

There was relief on her face, disproportionate to the small misunderstanding we'd just cleared up. She didn't want me to be lying, I sensed. She wanted everything between us to be out in plain view. Slowly, but inexorably, there was an atmosphere building up between us. A web of unspoken agreements, of multiple meanings of simple words, a whole aura of intimacy totally at odds with the bare facts of our brief acquaintance. To my relief, she stepped outside it first.

'Oh I see, Monkton City. That was why Harvey Robbins came in.'

I came back to reality on the run.

'My mind slows down in the evenings,' I told her. 'Just what has Harvey Robbins in common with Monkton?'

She looked, to satisfy herself I wasn't joking.

'Why that's where he comes from. You didn't know?'

'No, I didn't know.'

Louise had lost me now. I was clear of the web, my mind racing back and forth over what I knew, trying to see whether this new piece of information slotted in.

'Tell me about Mr. Robbins,' I invited.

She made a moue of disappointment.

'I didn't think you asked me out to hear a lot of tittle-tattle about the people I work with.'

I leaned over and touched her hand.

'You know very well I didn't, and we mustn't quarrel like a couple of kids. Believe me, this thing I'm working on is very important to somebody, and I can't afford to ignore any little piece of information I can get. As for us, this is not just a one-dinner encounter, not for me at least. We have time. Is that the way you feel about it?'

She nodded, almost shyly.

'It doesn't make any sense, does it? But I know what you mean. All right, if we're going to talk business talk, why are you so interested in Mr. Robbins?'

'I don't know,' I said honestly. 'But I started out from Monkton City. The case took me to Vale, and from Vale direct to L.A. Now, you wouldn't exactly call Los Angeles the smallest village on the West Coast, would you? So imagine my surprise when out of all the people here, the man who knows something about my problem, however little he knows, that man chances to hail from my own town?

Coincidence? Maybe. In fact, most probably. So, just to set my poor old mind at rest, let's establish that it is a coincidence, then I can forget it. Make sense?'

She listened seriously, no trace of banter in her voice when she replied.

'It makes sense. What did you want to know?'

That was just it. I hadn't the slightest idea.

'Well,' I began lamely, 'who is Mr. Robbins, for openers?'

She settled back in the chair, composed her hands neatly on her lap, and began to recite tonelessly.

'Robbins, Harvey Walter. Age 34. Graduate Monkton City Law Institute, first class pass. Special subjects, real estate and company law, state and federal. Joined firm, let's see, three, no, two and a half years ago. Salary—no, I don't think that's any of your concern.'

She looked across to see if I disagreed. I didn't.

'You're right, I'm not interested. What else about him, I mean what kind of a guy is he? Is he married for instance?'

'Not as far as I know. He lives alone, in an apartment down on the south side.'

'Is he a chaser?' I persisted.

Louise quirked her mouth in the beginnings of a smile.

'Well—er—'

'To be more specific,' I pressed. 'Has he

134

chased you?'

'Shall we say,' she returned, 'Mr. Robbins has indicated that he does not find me—er—repulsive.'

Good for Mr. Robbins. That was a point in his favor.

'O.K. so he's human. That's good. How does he pass his time?'

'I haven't the vaguest idea. He's a great one for joyriding of course.'

'How—joyriding? He's a little old isn't he?'

'I don't know what form it takes,' she admitted. 'But he seems to do an awful lot of driving. He was telling me the other week he wanted to trade in his car. The salesman said fifty thousand miles was a steep mileage for a two-year-old car.'

'The salesman was right,' I agreed. 'That's a lot of miles.'

And all in his leisure time. I didn't have a rundown on Harvey Robbins' work pattern, but I would guess his job didn't require him to do very much in the way of getting around. In that line of work, people come to you.

'You know,' said Louise, 'now that you put a question to me bluntly, I suddenly find I don't want to know too much about Harvey. He's a nice sort of man, always pleasant and friendly—'

I'll bet, I thought—

'—he's a hard worker, and a good one too. Punctual, doesn't drink too much at these awful social occasions we have to attend at times. No, I can't say a word against the man. When you come to weigh it all up, I don't really know much about him. It's not much help is it?'

I smiled encouragingly.

'Never mind, it's the kind of information I wish I got every day. Precise, factual, no emotional coloring. With some people, I'd have had to talk for an hour to wind up with the same facts.'

'Thank you sir, she said.' Louise inclined her head in acknowledgement. 'Have I done enough singing now? I mean, could we get down to the part where I get my supper? I'm ravenous.'

'Waiter,' I called.

Some women, especially women on a first date, put on such a display of being feminine and fragile, it's amazing they have enough strength to lift a knife and fork. They pick at their food, toy with minute portions, sigh delicately when offered a further serving. Louise Peters was not of that category. Right from the iced melon onward, she sat in there like a cowboy at the trail-end barbecue. From time to time, I tried a little light conversation, but she made it clear early in the proceedings that this was serious business, not to be interspersed with frivolities.

Gradually, I withdrew from the battle. She didn't need any help from me. They could line

136

up those dishes if they wanted, pile them high with daunting helpings, but nothing deterred Louise. This girl was in a class by herself. How anybody could eat like that, and retain the svelte shape opposite me was a minor mystery. She had the waiters eating out of her hand too. Metaphorically, that is. I don't believe she could have actually spared any of the food itself. But they fussed around, even bringing messages from the chef. Finally, when she reached her triumphant end, the head waiter scuttled away, returning with the chef in person, a huge barrel of a man, beaming all over his face. His name was Antonio.

Louise received him graciously, making expert comments on each course, and Antonio was her slave for life. He noticed me, in a face-in-the-crowd kind of way, but his eyes and his heart were all for Miss Peters. She allowed him to kiss her hand, then dismissed him regally.

'Is it always like this?' I queried.

'Oh no. Sometimes I hardly eat at all. You see,' she continued roguishly, 'it's only when something very unusual happens. Something to do with hormones. I have an odd balance, so my doctor tells me. If I'm moved over something the cortisone reacts on the adrenalin and the hormones, or perhaps it's the other way round. Come to think of it, I'm not at all certain just what does happen. But it happens all right. You can see that.'

She waved a nonchalant hand at the empty

137

dishes.

'It certainly does, lady, I'll vouch for that. But this is all very interesting,' I pursued. 'What is the particular something which has brought about this imbalance?'

She shook her head.

'I haven't the faintest idea,' she denied. 'And you can wipe off that self-satisfied smirk.'

We sat around a while, doing the coffee and liqueurs bit. Los Angeles has always been a happy town for me, and never happier than that evening with Louise Peters. We broke it up around ten, and I took her back to a small but elegant apartment. There, we talked of this and that in a half-hearted fashion, then we cut out the talking altogether. It was almost midnight when she pushed me away suddenly.

'No,' and the chestnut hair swirled as she shook her head. 'I'm not a prig, don't misunderstand me. But no matter how I feel at this moment it's too soon. I know hardly anything about you. Are you mad?'

I got my breathing back to where it was normal enough to permit me to speak.

'No,' I said regretfully. 'No, I'm not mad. There'll be other times.'

She placed a soft hand on my cheek and kissed me very gently.

'Thank you, Mark. Are you staying in town tonight?'

I realized suddenly I hadn't made any arrangements. Still, it wasn't too far to drive.

'No, I'd better get back. Have to call my client in the morning. When will I see you again?'

'As soon as you like,' she replied simply. 'Come to think of it, I haven't swum for ages. I hear there's some swimming water out your way?'

'A piece,' I admitted. 'I scarcely ever go down there myself. Maybe it's about time I corrected that. Let's see, it's Friday tomorrow. Do you work on Saturdays?'

'Sometimes. Not this one, though. And I could probably leave an hour early tomorrow evening. How would it be if I met you somewhere at around eight o'clock?'

'It would be,' I assured her, 'a very fine idea.'

I gave her telephone numbers, office and home, and addresses to go with them.

'Just in case there's any delay, on your part or mine, best if you call me when you get to town. If I'm going to get involved in anything myself, I can call you at the office?'

'Yes. But not later than four thirty.' She smiled that mysterious smile of hers, 'I can stay till late Sunday, if you're not tied up.'

It was a question. It didn't need to be.

'Lady,' I promised, 'I will be untied, and fast.'

It seemed to be what she wanted to hear. After that we didn't talk for a while, then when that old steam heat began to rise again we broke away. Louise took my jacket from the back of the chair where I'd thrown it.

'Good heavens, what have you got in here? It feels like a ton weight.'

She patted at the left shoulder, and the banter went out of her voice.

'It's a gun, isn't it? I hate guns.'

I took the coat from her, and slipped it on. I said seriously:

'No need to worry about guns honey. They're just tools, like pens or wrenches or whatever. They can be used, they can be misused. It isn't their fault.'

She shook her head quickly, in dismissal.

'Not as easy as that. Ordinary people don't find it necessary to carry those things.'

'Ordinary people don't run into the kind of characters I do, in the course of my lawful pursuits,' I told her gently. 'And don't forget, the law says I can have one. I have a permit, and they're not easy to come by.'

She wanted to be convinced, but her mind was still uneasy.

'Of course. I'm being silly. Let's forget it.'

Which wasn't what she meant at all. What she meant was, let's not talk about it any more, which is a very different thing. The gun had introduced a jarring note between us, and she didn't again recover her light-heartedness of a few minutes before. At the door we kissed more like old friends than the way it had been earlier.

'You'll be there tomorrow?' I pressed.

She nodded.

'I'll be there—'

I wasn't convinced, but I'd have to be satisfied with that. Out in the street I looked up at the large pale moon, and climbed regretfully into the Chev. The .38 seemed to be banging at my shoulder more than usual reminding me of the changed attitude of Louise Peters. I resolved to put her out of my mind, spend the journey back thinking about what I was going to tell Mrs. Erasmus Carter Junior in the morning. On the whole, I decided I hadn't been able to do much for her. I was in the middle of a very promising investigation, but all it promised was the clearing up of a few aged mysteries. I'd be fooling both my client and myself if I thought for one second I was any closer to finding Anthea Horan. Much as I disliked the idea of quitting, I'd have to advise Mrs. Carter she was probably wasting her money if she continued the investigation.

Not that my thinking was as concentrated as it ought to be. All the while I was trying to devote myself to the business in hand thoughts of Louise would intrude. I would smell again that elusive perfume, feel the soft brushing of that magic hair against my face. Such things have no contact with murder, and ex-convicts, and all the other little aspects of what I had called my lawful pursuits.

141

When I finally reached Monkton, I was dog-tired and low in spirits. Fortunately there was a bottle in the apartment that wasn't so low and I consoled myself with a large sample of the contents before opening the envelope which had been slipped under the door. It was from Florence Digby, the girl who runs the office, and me too when I'm there. I read:

Mr. Preston,
  Telephone call from Mrs. Erasmus Carter Junior
  Mrs. Carter will be away from the ranch until tomorrow afternoon. Will you please delay telephoning until after lunch, preferably at around four o'clock. I thought it best to deliver the message in case you did not come to the office again tomorrow.

Florence Digby

I chuckled. Some things don't change. There's the Statue of Liberty, the Pacific Ocean, my luck with the horses. And there's La Digby. That was a typical gibe of hers' that last part about if I did not come in again tomorrow. She was always like that, chasing me around, criticizing, complaining about my lack of attention to office routine.

Well, if Mrs. Carter didn't want a report until mid-afternoon, maybe I could have a few more hours looking for Anthea in the morning. Or rather, the same morning. It was already close to three a.m.

CHAPTER TEN

I didn't sleep too well, and was around before eight next morning. Sitting huddled over a cup of coffee, I stared into the steaming black depths and brooded. There was something about this whole business that had a cracked note when you rang it. That was one of the reasons I'd slept badly, turning the thing over and over in my mind, pawing at it, sniffing it. One conclusion I had reached was that I had a problem. In undertaking a simple search for a missing girl, or now woman, I'd uncovered a lot of interesting though apparently unconnected information. That information ought properly to be in police hands, and I was going to have to make up my mind whether to tell them or not. And even if I decided to tell them, which department did I tell? The thing started in Monkton City, true enough. But it ended so far in Los Angeles. And there was an interim stopover in Vale City, where one Lieutenant Franks had already said I was to keep in touch. Not forgetting that Ben Fawcett of the Monkton department had made similar sounds.

I find it tough enough to think clearly any

morning, but a morning following less than five hours of disturbed sleep is especially muddy. I gave the coffee pot some more action and smoked a couple of cigarets. Things were getting clearer all the time. The way I was seeing it now, this was really Vale police business. All they knew about James Earnshaw was that he'd been murdered on their territory. I knew who he was, or almost certainly. They didn't know about the tie-in between Earnshaw, Judson and the A.B. Amusements company. I did. I also knew, or thought I did, that Robert M. Stone was discouraging people, especially people with private buzzers, from looking into all these interesting old facts. Maybe Stone had killed Earnshaw/Judson, and maybe not. But he certainly knew many things he wasn't going to tell me. And he might be persuaded to tell the police, because they can get awful persuasive about things like that, particularly when there is a hint of murder in the background.

As I say, it was all very fascinating, and it might be of some value to the boys over in Vale. I couldn't really see that any of it was likely to lead me to Anthea Horan, so it was time for me to duck out. I put in a call to Vale.

'Lieutenant Franks please.'

'Franks.'

'Oh this is Mark Preston. I'm in Monkton City at the minute, but you said if I found anything interesting?'

He said cheerily:

'Oh Preston. Yes, well, I never refuse information. What've you got?'

I started to tell him, and he became very interested.

'Look,' he interrupted, 'this sounds like good red meat, all this. You've been busy, and I appreciate your calling. I suppose you wouldn't be able to find time to get over here and make a proper statement? I realize it's well off your beat, but I'd certainly appreciate it.'

Well, I reasoned, I'd half known he was going to ask that when I made the call.

'Sure, lieutenant, tell you what, I'll come over now. I just have one small call to make here in town, then I could be with you at say eleven?'

'Just a minute. Eleven you say. No, I have some people coming in then. Would twelve suit you?'

'Twelve it is. Say, does the department allow a man a glass of beer on a sultry morning? I was thinking I'll need one after the drive. How about the Tinklebell? We could do the statement later.'

He thought about it, but not for long.

'Well, being as you'll be going to all this trouble for the benefit of the department, I imagine we could stretch a rule. I'll meet you there.'

We cut off with sounds of mutual esteem.

My mind was getting clearer all the time, and I even had the germ of an idea back there some place. I got dressed and went out. The call I intended to make was on Mr. Tubby Tuborg. He'd had about enough time now to nurse his bruises, and if this embryo idea was going to have any substance to it, Tuborg was the man to pump it in. I drove down to the firetrap he lived in, locking every door of the car carefully before leaving it. Then I tramped up to where I'd last talked with the fat man, although he hadn't known it at the time.

There was no answer to the first two knocks, so I kicked at the door hard. It wasn't the kind of door where an extra kick or so made much difference to its appearance.

'Whaddya want?'

A fearful voice came through the panels.

'Open up Tuborg. Police,' I barked gruffly.

'Police? Oh.'

Fingers scrabbled at a rusty chain and the door began to open. I put weight against it before he could see who it was.

'Hey,' he protested, falling back. 'You get outta here.'

'In a minute,' I said pleasantly.

Closing the door behind me, I carefully put the chain back into position. Tuborg had retreated to the window, and watched this performance with a worried frown.

'Listen,' he pleaded. 'Be a good guy and leave me alone. I could get into all kinds—'

He broke off suddenly, realizing what he was saying.

'Go ahead. Finish it,' I invited. 'You could get into all kinds of trouble if what? If certain people knew you were talking to me? Tell me about the people, Tubby. I'm very fond of people. What kind of people?'

His back was against the wall now, and he had no further to retreat. Staring at me sullenly, he said:

'I got nothing to say.'

'Come on Tubby, don't be so modest. Sure you have. You have lots to tell me, and then we'll tell the law.'

'Law?' He looked up quickly. 'Nah, cut it out. You ain't gonna tell the law nothing. That's just talk.'

'We'll see,' I promised grimly. 'Say, whatever happened to you? Somebody else doesn't like you, huh?'

He put a flabby hand instinctively to the black and yellow bruises on his face. There was a strip of plaster down one cheek, too.

'Mind your own damn business,' he growled.

I looked at him with disgust. He'd evidently crawled from bed to answer the door. The grimy shirt flapped outside his creased pants, and the zipper had failed to overcome the fat bulge at his middle. He hadn't shaved for a couple of days, and according to my nose, there hadn't been a lot of contact with any soap either.

147

'The place stinks,' I announced. 'You stink, too. Don't they have any water in the place?'

'Ritz is two blocks along,' he returned. 'I do what I please.'

I nodded, taking out an Old Favorite and lighting it. His eyes were on the pack, but I didn't offer it around. I puffed clouds of gray smoke around, letting it fight the stifling atmosphere.

'That's interesting, about you doing what you please,' I assured him chattily. 'But you don't always please everybody else, I guess.'

He watched me through narrowed eyes, hating me and knowing he was powerless to do anything about me.

'How about the guys who worked you over?' I asked. 'Did you please them too?'

'That was personal. I got in an argument with the wrong people. These things happen. It's my business.'

He was scared, the fat man. Scared of what I might do, that much was obvious. But I had a feeling he was much more afraid of what I might get out of him.

'Personal, eh? Well you should be more careful how you talk to a lady. Or about a lady.'

I said the last part very slowly, so he didn't miss the import. It took him by surprise, and understanding showed fleetingly on the thick face before he recovered himself. A large soft tongue ran along the rubber lips before he spoke.

'Look Preston, I don't know what you want. But this I tell you. Whatever it is, you got the wrong address. I don't know nothing. I don't see nothing, I don't say nothing. All right, maybe you give me a little work out. I won't like it, but I'll take it. A few belts in the mouth is nothing new to me. But you'll get nothing.'

'My, my. Aren't we tough today. You're sure you can make it stick?'

I moved threateningly towards him and he shrank back, drawing in breath sharply.

'Go ahead,' he said resignedly. 'It won't do you any good.'

And there was that about him, an air of helpless resolution, which told me it was true.

'You have me wrong, fat boy. I didn't come here to hurt you. I came to do you a favor.'

Seeing that I wasn't going to attack him, at least for the moment, a little confidence seeped back into his bearing.

'Help me,' he scoffed. 'You wanta help me, I'll tell you what you do. You back around, go through that door, and don't ever talk to me again. This is the kind of help I want from you.'

I shook my head and grinned.

'You don't understand at all. I'm here to keep the police off your back.'

It was his turn to shake his head.

'I don't go for that. I ain't in no trouble with the law. And even if I ever was, how come they

149

let you get to me first? It ain't the kind of service they usually provide.'

'Ah no, you're right.'

I made a small performance out of cleaning up a chair so I could sit down.

'You're right, Tubby. But that's where I come in. You see, I'm the one who goes to the police. I tell them about you.'

He waved a hand in heavy dismissal.

'Tell 'em what? I didn't do nothing.'

'Maybe,' I agreed. 'But the way I'll tell it, it'll certainly sound like it.'

'All right captain, what's the beef? Did I park under a No Wait sign? Or maybe a hydrant?'

'No, no. This is a little more serious. The name of the game is murder.'

'M— You're screwy.' He actually recovered himself so far as to laugh. 'Boy, you really blew one. Murder? Anybody in town'd laugh at that.'

I didn't join in the laugh. Looking at him seriously I said:

'Oh I don't mean you actually murdered anybody personally. But you knew about it, had a connection with it. And you didn't tell anyone what you knew, especially the police. You're what they call an accessory to murder. After the fact. Maybe before the fact, too. Oh, you're in it. Should be worth say four to six. Five to seven with a tough judge.'

He moved away from the wall and stood

150

looking down at me. The puzzlement on his face was genuine.

'Mister, you have lost your marbles,' he said wonderingly. 'Just exactly what is all this?'

'We talked about your old buddy, Judson. Remember?'

'What about him?'

'You were one of the first people he looked up when he came out of jail.'

'And?'

'And he told you he was in the chips. About to clean up. He also told you he was going to Vale City.'

'What about it? Lots of guys go to Vale City.'

I nodded sympathetically.

'That's true. But lots of guys do not go there and get themselves bumped off. Judson did.'

Again he shook the great head.

'Did he now? Well suppose he did. It hadn't got nothing to do with me. I ain't seen the man in two years or better.'

'Think back to the good old days of Studio Six,' I suggested. 'Back when three people ran it. There was Judson, a man named Stone—'

His eyes flickered at the mention of Stone's name.

'—and there was a woman. Her name was Clara Jean Dollery.'

But he was ready for that name, and the heavy features remained impassive.

'When the law found out what was going on

151

at the studio, they moved in and grabbed the two men. They would have grabbed the Dollery woman too, only she skipped out in time. I wonder where she went, Tubby?'

'Search me,' he shrugged.

'It won't be necessary. She went to Vale City. When Judson came out of jail, and this was several months after Stone got out, he wanted to see Clara Jean. He wanted his cut. He went there, but what he got was a lot of lead in his belly.'

I smiled at Tuborg, but his face was white.

'There wasn't nothing in the papers,' he said doggedly.

'Yes there was, but not about Judson. You see, in Vale he was calling himself Earnshaw, James Earnshaw. There was a Mrs. Earnshaw too, but nobody ever saw her after the murder.'

'None of this is my concern,' repeated Tuborg. 'Earnshaw, Mrs. Earnshaw, who are these people? I never heard of them.'

'I don't believe you. I believe you tipped off somebody that Judson was on his way over there. That way they were ready for him. And after they knocked him off, you still didn't tell the police what you knew. That puts you in it.'

It wasn't good enough to persuade him, and it didn't. He let out a deep sigh, turning finally into a short laugh.

'Brother, you have an imagination. You really do. I woulda thought you was a pretty smart feller, but you don't imagine all this garbage is gonna stand up with the law boys do you? Why, there ain't a rookie with two days on the force would try to make a charge out of all that crap. There ain't a justice in town would sign a warrant. Who you kidding, Preston?'

I nodded patiently.

'I think you're probably right. I really do.'

'Well then, what—'

'But,' I persisted, 'you didn't let me finish. Here we have some nice complicated crime, it's all tangled and mixed up. The police haven't had a whole helluva lot to work on, so far. If I go down there and pitch a good line, and believe me I can tell a very fancy story when I try, they will at the very least want to talk to you, right?'

He shrugged flabbily.

'Talk, schmalk, let 'em. I talked to the law before. Those guys ain't dumb. Five minutes with me, and they'll see right off they got nothing to work with. Go tell 'em. Have yourself a ball.'

'Are you ever going to let me finish?' I demanded. 'So there you are trotting into headquarters to answer a few questions. And I just happen to telephone certain people and tell them to watch the place if they want a pleasant surprise. What are those people going to make of it if they see you there?'

He thought about that, and he didn't like it

too well. But he managed to persuade himself not to worry.

'Nah,' he decided. 'I could explain it. Everybody knows I don't look for trouble. I wouldn't be so dumb as to go to no cops.'

'But people sometimes can't afford to take chances, Tubby. Especially when it says in the papers, "Surprise witness in murder case", and there's a good clear picture of you. I have friends, good friends on most papers. A plant like that wouldn't be hard to arrange. Could you explain that one too?'

The newfound confidence was leaking away rapidly now.

'I don't get it,' he admitted. 'All that, a load of bananas to the cops, a phoney story in the sheets, you'd do all that to me? I mean, why would a man go to such a helluva lot of trouble just to get me in dutch with certain parties? What'd I ever do to you?'

'Nothing,' I assured him cheerfully. 'And it's no trouble. I just happen to be that kind of guy. As a child I cut up worms. But don't you go upsetting yourself, Tubby. I'm in no hurry. Half the fun is waiting while you suffer. I'll give you till tomorrow morning at ten. If you think of anything I might like to know by that time, I'm in the book. If you don't we'll start our little game.'

I got up, nodding to the frightened face.

'Well, I mustn't keep you. I know you have a lot to think about. Ciao Tubby.'

154

I left him there and went back to the sunshine. That's the trouble with this business. A man is forever going around shouting at people, making loud noises, scaring people. Little people, like Tubby Tuborg. I didn't really imagine he knew too much about the whole affair, but there was something. Some little thing he knew, probably without any guilty involvement, but which would help me slide one more piece of the puzzle into its place. And I had to have that something. Whatever it was, it was important enough for certain people to give him the hard word the night before, and if it worried them to that degree, it certainly interested me.

Over the years you develop your own way of going about things. And you learn. One of the first things you have to learn is that people, even innocent people, never tell you the whole truth. Even if they tell what they imagine to be the truth, it's heavily angled according to the way they see it. Sooner or later, like now, you reach a point where there isn't any new avenue to explore. When that happens you have two choices. One is to give it up, tell the client you're sorry, and charge them half-fare. That choice I don't like too well. The other alternative is to go back over the same territory you already covered, and make noises. Make lots of noises, threats, hints, half-veiled accusations, guesses. If you're lucky, you get somebody worried. Worried enough to make a move, and then it's up to you to spot that move, and it could be the very one which will give you what you want.

I'd started off by making noises with Tuborg, but I didn't have time to sit around and wait for any results that might produce. There were others to be visited, and next on the list was Robert M. Stone.

The outer door of the Red Pig was locked when I tried it, and I had a quick grin at the new notice which had been fixed to the door. Good. If Stone took me seriously over that, maybe he'd be willing to listen to some more. I walked down the narrow alleyway leading to the side entrance of the place. The heavy door opened at a touch and I stepped into almost total darkness which intensified as I pulled the door behind me. I listened, but there were no sounds. Then I stopped cold as a heavy gun went off, once, twice. Pulling the .38 from my jacket I edged cautiously forward. There was another thunderous crash, a door flung open and someone walked quickly away. I reached the open door of Stone's office, and a quick look inside told me the story. Faster now I ran to the door leading into the club, and opened it. A gun went off, lead slammed into the wall by my head. I dropped to the ground fired a couple of useless shots into the darkness. I knew it was hopeless. I wasn't going through that door, and the other man would know it. I'd be like a duck in a shooting gallery framed

156

in the light from the office. Shutting the door I turned back to Stone. My second look only confirmed the first. He was sprawled across the desk as though he'd risen from the chair, maybe to grab the gun. His eyes were open, and already glazing. There was no sign of any wound and he looked almost like a drunk who'd passed out. But I knew there were probably three big holes in the front of him, and he wouldn't look so pretty when the medics moved him from the table.

There was an open safe in the wall, and it was empty. So the motive could be robbery, but I doubted that. The coincidence was just too much for me to swallow. Quickly I went through the drawers in the desk, but there was nothing of interest, just papers to do with the running of the club. His side pockets were empty too. I couldn't get at his inside pockets without disturbing the body, and it was too much of a risk that the police would know I'd done it. There was nothing in the office. Nothing but death for Robert M. Stone and trouble for a certain Preston. Then I noticed something. The picture was gone. On my last visit to Stone I'd noticed a photograph of a woman on the desk. It wasn't there now. That might mean something and nothing, but it was worth noting.

Reluctantly I picked up the phone and dialled a familiar number. People jumped around at the other end as I sang my song, and

I was ordered to stay where I was. As if I didn't know. I replaced the receiver, and lit an Old Favorite. I wished Stone would close his eyes. Wherever I stood he seemed to be staring at me, accusing me for not arriving two minutes earlier, so he might have a chance of still being alive. I turned my back on him and smoked jerkily.

'Put up your hands, and gently.'

The command came from behind, and the voice was soft. I went very cold, and my spine twitched. If this was the man who killed Stone, I might not even get to finish the cigaret.

'Turn around.'

I didn't want to turn round. I knew what heavy caliber bullets do to a man's stomach, and I didn't want any first-hand experience. The man standing in the doorway was the character who'd tried to stop me from seeing Stone on my last visit. And the gun in his hand was a .32. Some of my courage came back, not all. The shots that killed Stone had been fired from a much heavier weapon.

'Ah, it's you,' he purred. 'I had a feeling we hadn't seen the last of you. Mr. Stone would appear to be dead.'

Whatever other feelings this guy might have, he wasn't about to bust out crying over his late boss.

'That would be my bet,' I agreed.

'And you would appear to be here,' he went on, in the same casual tone.

I made a half-bow.

'Please don't do that again,' he entreated. 'I'm of a naturally nervous disposition, and I might have to kill you for my own safety. In fact, I have to admit, it would be a pleasure.'

He smiled, and I realized I'd read him wrong the last time around. I'd dismissed him too lightly, and the confident way he'd held the gun told me it was a familiar pose.

'Now wait a minute—' I began.

'I'll do the talking,' he snapped. 'I don't care about Stone. But there was close to fourteen thousand dollars in that safe. I'm only guessing of course, but it would be my guess the money is no longer there. Where is it?'

'You'd have to ask whoever killed him,' I suggested.

'Come now, I don't have all day. Are you saying you didn't do this?'

I couldn't make up my mind whether he was pulling a big double bluff. If he'd killed Stone, he'd have had plenty of time to get rid of the money and the murder weapon, then come back in with another gun and a surprised expression. But if I could keep him talking, the police would arrive at any minute.

'No, I didn't kill him. Whoever did it left here not three minutes ago, and you must have passed them on your way in. You have a key to the front door?'

'Sure, I have a key. I'm—' then he stopped, frowning. 'Wait a minute, don't you ask me

159

questions. I'm not the one who got found with a murdered man.'

'No,' I agreed. 'But you are the one with the gun.'

'What of it? It hasn't been fired in days. Anyway, who said he was shot? I don't see any holes.'

'They're in the front,' I explained. 'As though you didn't know.'

'As though—' he stopped again. 'If you know he's been shot in front, could I ask how you know?'

'Sure. I heard the gun go off. Guy took a shot at me, too.'

'We'll see how the police like your story,' he sneered.

'They'll like it,' I assured him. 'I've nothing to hide from the police.'

'That's good,' said a new voice. 'We like people who don't have anything to hide. How about putting down that gun, mister?'

CHAPTER ELEVEN

We both looked and there was Randall leaning nonchalantly in the doorway. But there was nothing nonchalant about the Police Special in his hand.

'Welcome Gil, and I mean it.'

The other man quickly lowered the .32, and

made to put it in his pocket.

'Uh uh,' said Randall. 'I'll kind of look after that for a while. Butt first, you understand.'

He took the thirty-two, and sniffed at the snout. Schultz had materialized beside him, and Randall handed him the gun.

'Not been fired,' he reported. 'All right, Preston, who's your friend?'

'My name is Royal, Henry Royal.'

'Fine, fine.'

Randall stumbled across to stare down at the dead man's face.

'Stone, eh? Who did it?'

Neither Royal nor I had any answer to that one. Randall poked around the room for a few seconds.

'Was he like this when you found him?' he asked me.

'Exactly like that. I've touched nothing.'

'Fine, fine. Seems I recall you have a permit to carry a gun. Where would it be?'

'In my pocket.'

'Well don't be coy about it Preston. Hand it over.' Silently, I passed him the .38. Again he went through his sniffing routine, and this time he made a face.

'Not so good. Somebody's been shooting this thing off. I guess they must have used it on Stone, then slipped it back in your pocket without you noticing.'

'I took a couple of bangs at the killer,' I told him. 'You'll find the slugs somewhere out

161

there.'

'Maybe.'

Randall leaned back against the desk, oblivious to the corpse a few inches away from his hand.

'All right, let's hear the fairy tale.'

I told him what happened. Schultz scribbled quickly at his little pad.

'And that's all?' demanded Randall.

'That's all,' I confirmed.

'How 'bout you, Mr. Royal? You agree with Preston here?'

Royal shook his head.

'I can't say anything about what happened earlier. But from the time I arrived, yes that part is true.'

'Fine, fine. Look at all this corroborated evidence we're getting around here. The only little piece we don't have is the bit about who rubbed out this guy on the desk. Any thoughts about that?'

'I know nothing about that,' denied Royal. 'It was all over before I arrived.'

'Then you've nothing to worry about, I'm sure. Somebody's been a little careless with that safe door, wouldn't you say. Was there anything in there?'

Royal bit his lip, and hesitated.

'Come on now Mr. Royal,' cajoled Randall. 'An innocent man doesn't have to worry about the truth.'

'There was money, a lot of money.'

'That's better. Just how much, would you say?'

'A little under fourteen grand, so Stone told me last night.'

Randall pursed his lips in a small whistle.

'So? That seems an awful lot to have around for a place this size. I would have thought five, six hundred would be all the cash needed here at any one time. Would you have thought that Mr. Royal?'

'I thought so, yes.'

'Why do you suppose the late Mr. Stone should have that much cash lying around? Do you normally take that much in an evening?'

Royal sniffed, and shook his head.

'We certainly do not. Nor in a week either. I don't know why Stone should have had it here.'

Randall nodded thoughtfully.

'Well, it seems he did. If he did, why would he want to tell you about it, Mr. Royal? I mean, I'm sure he trusted you and all that, but why would he want to tell you? He was asking for trouble wasn't he? Did he go out in the club, and make an announcement or something?'

'You see, the fact is—was —'

Royal faltered and stopped. Schultz looked up over his pencil. Randall said patiently:

'The fact is or was what?'

'Stone was clearing out. I wasn't supposed to tell anybody. He was planning on leaving this morning. I was to take over here as manager for the new owner.'

'Ah. And who would that be?'

'I don't know. Stone told me he'd fixed it all up for me to get the job. The new owners would be in touch today.'

'Uh huh. And this money then, this was the selling price, you imagine?'

Royal shrugged.

'I don't know. I wouldn't have known about any of it, only I happened to come into the office while Stone was stacking up these piles of bills in the safe. That's when he told me.'

Randall nodded, as though satisfied.

'Well let's come back to that later. You Preston, what're you doing here? Just one of your routine calls to see if there are any killings today?'

'I don't want to say too much in front of this character,' I replied. 'Could we talk outside?'

Randall stared at me carefully for several seconds.

'I guess that could be arranged,' he agreed. 'Ah, here comes the rest of the squad.'

And in tropped the usual menagerie of photographers, fingerprint artists, the whole caboodle of scientific backing for the homicide squad.

'We'd be better off out of the way, Mr. Royal,' suggested Randall.

'Let's all go out in the club if we can find some lights.'

164

We moved out of the office and Royal snapped down switches. Soft lights flooded the darkness, and I peered around quickly in case the gun-artist was lurking in the club.

'Kinda jumpy today, aren't you?' grumbled Randall.

'Uh uh,' I denied. 'It's just this skin trouble I have. I'm allergic to holes in it.'

The sleepy eyes looked me over.

'That was on the level, that stuff in there?'

He jerked his head in the direction of the office.

'Absolutely,' I confirmed.

'So let's hear the rest of it. What's so secret we don't want Royal to know about it?'

'You know Ben Fawcett? He has Fraud and Morals over at the Fourth Precinct?'

'I know him. You saying he did this?'

'You know I'm not. But he was interested in Stone. Told you so.'

Randall digested this information, made little of it.

'Why would he tell you? Or do the Fourth Precinct send you a mimeograph of current affairs once a week?'

I knew I was going to have to tell Randall in the end. He might not like it very much, but he'd like it a lot less if I held out on him. Reluctantly I began my recital. I kept it brief, leaving out one or two things. It wouldn't do for Randall to know as much as me, because with his organization he'd probably get results

165

quicker, and that wouldn't suit me at all. When I got to the end he said:

'H'm.'

After that, he didn't say anything at all for a full minute.

'H'm. You're a busy little feller, aren't you? And you dug out all this old stuff, just looking for this fugitive from Sunnybrook Farm?'

The tone was as sceptical as the words.

'It wasn't hard,' I assured him. 'I mean, I didn't turn up any buried treasure or hidden wills or such. It was all routine enquiry work.'

'Maybe. And now, what do you make of this Stone deal? You think maybe somebody decided you were getting too close? Stone may have given something away, and he was better off dead? That how you stack it up?'

I shook my head.

'I doubt it, Gil. Too complicated. Why Stone? He was one of the bunch, if there is a bunch. It would be much more logical, wouldn't it, to give me the treatment? Always supposing I am close to anything. And that there's anything to get close to.'

'Sounds reasonable,' he admitted grudgingly. 'How 'bout this guy Eldridge? Anything there?'

'Maybe. I really don't doubt there's any connection between Stone's murder and my little investigation. After all, there's a small matter of fourteen grand involved. That's a good enough motive for murder in anybody's

166

book.'

Again the heavy eyes inspected me.

'You sure you didn't knock him off for the dough? If so, I'd be very grateful if you'd tell me. This chilblain of mine is shouting its head off today.'

'Sorry,' I denied. 'I'd like to help you out Gil, and your chilblain too, but it just isn't my kind of party.'

He sighed noisily.

'I was afraid of that. O.K. let's get down to the office and sweat out a statement.'

'Er,' I demurred.

He looked at me quickly.

'Er, I was wondering would you mind if I left it till later?'

He clapped me on the shoulder with a hand like a side of beef.

'Why, certainly not. Of course we don't mind. I'd hate you to think the department would wish to interfere with your private life. I mean, how would it look if we started bothering the public with our unimportant little murders? Drop in any old time. Would next month be convenient?'

'Don't be that way, Gil. It's just that I promised another policeman I'd give him a statement this morning.'

He grunted sourly.

'What other policeman?' he demanded.

'Lieutenant Franks, over in Vale City. I told you about him just now.'

'That's on the level?'

'Check if you want. They have telephones.'

He treated me to another of his deep, helpless sighs.

'What a way to earn a living. All right, get in when you can.'

It was a dismissal, but I lingered.

'What're you waiting for?'

'It's the gun. I do have a license for it. And you know very well I didn't kill Stone.'

'Preston, you have the most almighty nerve. All the years I've known you, that nerve of yours gets worse, I swear.'

I grinned.

'Exactly. And all those years you've known me, tell you I didn't do it.'

Snorting derision, he dived into his pocket and pulled out the .38.

'Here. It's enough to cost me my badge. And don't forget that statement.'

He had to shout the last part, because I was hurrying out of the club before he changed his mind.

CHAPTER TWELVE

I dropped in at the office in case there was anything of importance in the mail. La Digby gave me her cold look, the one I get for being missing off the job.

'There's been a lady on the telephone. A Miss Peters?'

'Did she leave a message?'

'She asked if you would call her. I'm afraid I had to say I didn't know much about your movements.'

The last was a typical Digby gibe.

'It's a Los Angeles number. I'll look it up,' I offered.

'I have the number, thank you. Shall I get it now?'

Completely beaten into submission, I scuttled into my own office and waited. The phone blatted and I heard Louise.

'Mark? Look, I'm sorry, I won't be able to make it today.'

Disappointed, I said:

'That's too bad. You're not sick, are you?'

'Nothing like that, it's work I'm afraid. You remember the man you met yesterday? In Mr. Davis' office?'

'Robbins? Harvey Robbins?'

'Yes. Well, he hasn't shown up this morning, and it puts our schedule out. I'm sorry.'

Harvey Robbins. Ex Monkton City. Lawyer. The man who did the legal work for James Earnshaw. The one who rented Earnshaw an apartment.

'Mark, are you there?'

'Yes honey, I'm here. My mind is whirling around. Any message from Harvey? I mean about why he's not in the office?'

169

'Well, really,' and her tone was offended. 'I was hoping you might show a little human reaction. Such as disappointment, for example.'

'Oh I'm disappointed, of course I am. It's just that Harvey suddenly seems a very interesting fellow. What about that message?'

'If it's that important to you,' she said huffily, 'he telephoned to say some urgent personal business had come up, and he wouldn't be in before Monday.'

'Now that is very interesting.'

I was talking half to myself.

'Well good-bye Mr. Preston. If any more news comes to my knowledge about Mr. Robbins I'll be sure and contact you.'

'Hey now wait a minute.'

I pulled my mind quickly back to the important subject of Miss Louise Peters. It took several minutes to mollify her, and several more to establish that she would come the next day, Saturday. After putting down the phone, I sat still. For a while I was thinking about Louise Peters. It's a sign of weakness in my character, I guess. Somehow I always find I prefer to think about women than about murder and mayhem. But women don't pay the grocer, not in my case at least. So I pushed the warm memory of Louise from my mind and got back to Harvey Robbins. It could be something and nothing. But too many roads led back to Harvey, for me to be able to afford to ignore him.

According to Louise, Harvey had joined Davis' firm about two and a half years earlier. Anyone with an involved mind might remember that was about the time one Robert M. Stone came out of jail. I have exactly that kind of mind. Picking up the telephone again I called Shad Steiner.

'Oh, it's you,' he said unenthusiastically. 'Do I get that big story now?'

'I'm working on it,' I assured him. 'You heard about the murder at the Red Pig this morning?'

He snorted.

'Whaddya mean, heard about it? I had a man down there thirty minutes ago. Hey,' and his tone became suspicious, 'what do you know about that? It's red hot.'

'That's what I wanted to tell you,' I explained. 'I was there, practically saw it happen. And I won't talk to any other newspaper.'

'Well, this is better. This is what I call a return on my investment. Where are you?'

'Just on my way out of town. Now wait, wait. I'll talk to your boy later. You can even claim to have found the missing witness or something.'

'H'm,' he was doubtful. 'Out of town, you say? You didn't scrag this character yourself, did you?'

'Not this time. If I tell you something, do

171

you promise not to print it?'

'No. I print everything.'

'All right. Do you promise to hold it until you have the whole story. This thing is stirring up old memories. I wouldn't want your startling revelations to frighten people back into hiding. Not when they're just crawling out into the daylight.'

'Like that? Well, try me.'

'This Stone, the man who was killed this morning. He was one of the people put away for that dirty pictures rap down at Studio Six. The one you let me check your files on the other day.'

There was silence at the other end. Then he said:

'It's a good one, huh? You really got me a good one this time?'

'I hope so, Shad. It's early to be positive, but I hope so. Now I need one little thing.'

'Name it.'

'Have that little girl look in the file again. Tell me the name of the lawyer who defended Stone and Judson.'

'File's on its way,' he said laconically. 'I sent for it the second you mentioned Stone. Should be here about, let's see, five—four—three—two—ah. Hold it.'

There was the rustle of paper being turned over at the other end.

'You still there?'

'Yup.'

'Ryker. Wouldn't you know, it's always Ryker.'

I was disappointed, though I should have expected it.

'No mention of anyone else working with him at all.'

'No. I'm still checking through while we talk. No. No I guess not. That's it. It's no help, huh?'

'At least it cancels out a thought I've been playing with. Thanks anyway, Shad. I'll be sure and let you know the minute I get back.'

'Well just don't forget it. And don't go blabbermouthing to the competition.'

I assured him he needn't worry and hung up. After a moment's thought, I dialled another number.

'Ryker and Smart. Good morning.'

'Good morning. Like to speak to Mr. Robbins, please.'

'Mr. Robbins?'

The girl's voice was querulous.

'That's it, Mr. Harvey Robbins.'

'Just one moment, please.'

I stared at the ceiling and waited.

'Hallo. I'm sorry sir, but we don't have anyone by that name.'

'Are you sure?'

'Oh yes, I've checked.'

Before she could cut me off, I said quickly:

'That's too bad. I just arrived in town, and this is the number I always used to call. Mind,

I haven't been here in two or three years. Could be Mr. Robbins moved on. I wonder would you mind asking again.'

'Ah,' she said brightly. 'Now that could be it. I've only been here just a few months myself. If you'll hold on, I'll ask some of the other staff.'

Thare's nothing like holding a phone for focusing the attention. I counted eleven specks of dust on the otherwise immaculate surface of my desk. I even noticed a small pile of correspondence in one corner, which Florence Digby had put there in the hope I may get around to reading it some day.

'Are you there?'

'Yes.'

She sounded quite pleased with herself.

'You are absolutely right. Mr. Robbins was a junior lawyer here until two or more years ago. But I'm afraid he's left us.'

'Oh dear,' I sounded disappointed. 'This is a pity. I was hoping to see him again. You wouldn't have a forwarding address?'

'I'm sorry, no. I don't have access to the files without Mr. Ryker's personal permission. But one of the staff in the office remembers he was going to Vale City.'

Vale City. A great warm glow spread through me. I almost purred into the mouthpiece.

'Miss, I want to thank you very much for all your trouble.'

'No trouble at all. Hope you find him.'

174

And with more pleasantries we cut off. I rubbed my hands gleefully. Vale City again. Judson had come out of jail and headed straight for Vale City. Somebody there didn't like him and he got himself killed in that friendly little town. Harvey Robbins had been working in Monkton at the time of Judson's trial. As soon as I showed up and started asking questions, Robbins disappeared. Well all right, he hadn't disappeared, but he certainly went missing from his office. Robbins had also headed for Vale City on leaving Monkton. It was too much to hope that he'd be headed that way again, certainly too remote a possibility to justify my making a special trip. But I didn't have to. I was going there anyway to see Lieutenant Franks. I wouldn't be putting myself to any trouble at all by asking a few harmless questions while I was on the spot.

Minutes later I was back on that steaming highway again, whistling one of my timeless specials as the concrete strip unrolled. My collar got busy wilting, and glueing itself to the back of my neck, but I remained obstinately cheerful. By the time I wheeled into the immaculate forecourt of the Tinklebell, I was seriously in need of repairs by way of something that comes tall and cold. In a glass. I walked into the bar called Maggie's Place. The bartender was the same man I'd seen on my last trip.

'Howdy,' he greeted. 'Back again eh Mr.—

wait a minute—Mr. Porter.'

'Preston,' I corrected.

'Say, I'm sorry. Preston, that's right. What'll you have, Mr. Preston?'

I took the coldest beer on the shelf and sipped at it.

'That is very good,' I admitted. 'I just had a long ride to get here.'

'No day for rides,' he replied. 'Nossir, this is a day for cold beer and a quiet place. You're here.'

I offered to buy him a drink but he said it was too early. Taking the cold glass in my hand I wandered across to sit by a window. There weren't many people around and I enjoyed the peace of the place after the hot journey. I'd been there about ten minutes when a blue police sedan swung into view and parked. Franks got out, locking the doors carefully before coming in. He didn't spot me at once, caught me on the second look around. I waved and he came over, sticking out his hand.

'Sorry I'm late,' he greeted.

'That's O.K. This is some of the nicest shade in the state,' I told him. 'Let me get you a drink.'

He settled for beer, and to save a lot of walking around I got myself another while I was at the bar.

'See your friend Mr. Franks is here,' nodded the bar jockey. 'Haven't been speeding, have you?'

I muttered something equally fatuous in reply and carried the glasses across to where Franks had parked himself.

'Man, that looks good. In any civilized society, people would spend the whole summer drinking cold beer.'

'I'll drink to that,' I agreed.

He took a swallow, smacked his lips and sighed heavily.

'I want you to know I appreciate the trouble you're going to over this. Like to tell me about it?'

I'd been wondering how much I ought to tell him, and how much to keep to myself. Whether he appreciated my help or not, he was a law officer first and second, and if he decided that Monkton City ought to have all the facts I'd be cooling my heels in Randall's office for many a long hour.

'Well, it would seem I have a good lead on your friend Earnshaw, as I told you on the phone.'

'M'm. Tell me what you dug up.'

I kept it to Earnshaw at first, just dates and places. He listened attentively, nodding at each point I made.

'Sounds like my man,' he muttered. 'And your man, too. What do you make of it?'

'Damned if I know,' I said honestly. 'Now I have another complication. You remember I told you I had an idea the man might be looking for his cut of some deal or other?'

'Yes.'

'There were two other people involved. Man named Stone was one. He got convicted with Judson, or Earnshaw if you like. The other was a woman by the name of Clara Jean Dollery. She got away completely. I had it figured that Stone was the most likely person to have killed Judson.'

'Why?' he returned quickly. 'I told you how he died. Unless the guy was a fairy it would have to be a—oh. Oh, I get it. You're thinking this Dollery could have done it.'

'Maybe. But what I was going to tell you was that Stone has to be crossed off. In fact somebody crossed him off this morning.'

Franks took the glass away from cooling his forehead, and looked at me sharply.

'Ah. There has to be more.'

'There is. I had the pleasure of finding him.'

I went on to describe what had happened at the Red Pig a few hours before.

'What do you make of it now?' he queried.

I shrugged and emptied my glass.

'It's hard to know. Could be something and nothing. The easy answer is that as soon as I start raking up the past, things start to happen. But I'm not so sure it's the right answer. After all, Stone was a small-timer, close to the fast money. Guys like that make enemies every day. It's not been my experience that people want to live in the past. The Studio Six thing was years ago. Even the Judson murder was

178

two years back, and I think you'd agree it wouldn't be easy to get a conviction on it now. Every lead is stone cold. I wouldn't imagine it would be worth the risk of a brand new murder.'

'So you don't think the Stone killing is connected?' he asked.

I wagged my head in denial.

'I'm not saying that exactly. There could be a connection, but I doubt if it's caused by my poking around.'

The lieutenant wagged a finger.

'I don't get it. What is it you're saying exactly?'

'What I'm trying to say, and I don't seem to be doing it very well, is that if Stone has been killed in connection with all this old stuff, it's my guess he would have been killed whether I showed or not. I don't see why anything I'm liable to uncover would justify murder.'

'Except maybe your own,' contributed Frank. 'Had you thought about that?'

I lit an Old Favorite and a blue cloud hung lazily in front of my face.

'Yes, I thought about it,' I admitted. 'And it would make more sense, wouldn't it? Look it it this way. If a guy starts asking questions, he could make things dangerous for somebody. So what does the somebody do? He doesn't start killing other people, because that still leaves the man with the long nose. No, surely the sensible thing would be to knock him off.

179

That would finish it.'

'And nobody tried?'

'Not lately. Not on this caper. So, one way and another, I think Stone was eliminated for quite different reasons.'

'I see. I'll get another beer.'

He brought back new supplies and we sat in silence for a moment. Then he started asking me questions. He asked about Studio Six, and the cold trail I uncovered in Los Angeles.

'You seem to come across this Harvey Robbins every which way,' he remarked. 'And there's a kind of inflection in your voice when you refer to him. Something I should know about?'

'Something and nothing,' I agreed.

I told him of the tenuous connection I could establish between Robbins and my investigation at various points along the way.

'Not very convincing,' he demurred. 'Nothing very crooked about working in Monkton City, is there? And I don't find it very suspicious to have a lawyer involved with legal documents. I would tend to think that is the man's profession.'

He quirked his mouth as he spoke, and I realized he was ribbing me.

'Something similar occurred to me,' I admitted. 'Still, you know how it is on these investigations. If you're lucky, you get a feeling. I'm beginning to have one about Mr. Robbins. And I'd sure like to know where he is.'

Franks nodded, wiping foam from his mouth.

'I know the feeling. Sometimes it pays off. You have something else to tell me, don't you?'

Policemen, I sighed inwardly. Always that little jump ahead.

'Yes. It's my hunch, and I have nothing to justify it, that the woman, Clara Jean Dollery, came here to Vale City when the Studio Six affair blew up. I think it was she Judson came to see, and that's how he got himself killed. I think if Robbins is mixed up in this at all, he's either on his way or he's here already. I'd give a lot to find them.'

'Always supposing you're right,' he added.

'Always supposing I'm right.'

'H'm. And you want me to help you?'

I grinned at him quickly, and got the straightforward department blank stare in return.

'It had occurred to me.'

'Like to help you, Preston, I mean that, but look how hopeless it it. What have I got? I'm supposed to find a woman who may or may not have lived here about five years. Who may or may not be married by now, with a houseful of kids. Who will almost certainly have changed her name. Who doesn't have a decent description available, leave alone a photograph. We run a pretty good department here in Vale, that much I'll say. But we're a little under strength on the magic squad.'

I nodded. It was a fair answer, and about what I'd expected.

'How about Robbins? You think there's any chance of checking whether he was with a law firm here, or working with one?'

Franks exhaled deeply.

'Well, that's a little easier. We only have half a dozen lawyers in the city and most of them have been here years. Yes, I'll have that checked out.'

'Thanks, I'm obliged to you. Er—'

He got up resignedly, and shrugged.

'O.K. If it's that important to you, I'll go and phone the department now and get a man on it. Half a dozen calls won't take up much time, and I guess I owe you for the Earnshaw identification.'

He went away to find a telephone, and I gazed around at the people who had drifted in since we started talking. There was one girl, a large fruity young blonde, displaying plenty of firm tanned flesh. She was being very chummy with a not so young crewcut character, who would be better occupied in his office than sitting around in bars pawing at girls young enough to be his daughter. Or that was the way I saw it, at least. It's typical of my curious trade that I have to watch other guys fondling the juicy friendly blondes, while I chew the fat about murder and other pleasantries with police officers. A man could get a jaundiced view of life.

Then I saw Franks making his way back towards me. Well, this was more like it. He wasn't alone now. At his side, and listening intently to what he was saying, was a small vivacious brunette.

'Mr. Preston, like to have you meet Maggie Murphy. She owns the place.'

'Great pleasure, Miss Murphy.'

I meant it. She was about thirty or thirty-five and a considerable looker. The handshake was firm and friendly, and the gray eyes looked at me directly. As we shook hands something dug into my fingers. The something was an enormous emerald that would weigh several pounds by the look of it.

'Nice to have you here, Mr. Preston. Mac— that's the bartender, told me you left word the other day.'

'Yes, I'm sorry to have missed you. Especially now that I see you.'

Her eyes twinkled and she turned accusingly on Franks.

'You didn't tell me he was fellow-Irish.'

'I didn't know it,' returned Franks. 'Are you?'

'Afraid not,' I confessed.

'Nonsense,' she smiled. 'With that line of blarney you'll find there's some Irish back there someplace. Dig into the family records.'

'I'll go into it,' I promised. 'Say, forgive me.

183

Could I get you something to drink?'

'No thank you. I have rather a lot to do. Just wanted to meet you, being a friend of the lieutenant's here. Next time.'

'I'll look forward to it.'

The policeman and I sat down, watching her as she walked away.

'Wow,' I murmured. 'Thanks for thinking of me.'

'My pleasure,' he beamed. 'Maggie is nice, no?'

'Maggie is nice, yes,' I corrected. 'She must pull in the men in crowds.'

'She does,' he confirmed. 'And yet, you know, it's a funny thing, all the wives and girl friends like her, too. That's very unusual.'

'It is. You mean she hasn't cut across any wives or girl friends?'

'Not that I know of. As she puts it, this is her place of business. Her private life is for her private time. She doesn't lead the life of a recluse, that much I know. But she keeps all that in the background.'

I watched her talking to some men at the bar, caught the sudden flash of her smile. Like I do with every good-looking dame I meet, I had the feeling I'd seen her before.

She must have felt my eyes on her, because she turned suddenly and caught me staring. At once, I looked away and stared out the window. Franks chuckled.

'Serves you right. You've seen an attractive

woman before.'

'True. I just had a feeling I've seen that particular one before today.'

A small red Italian sports job swung crazily into the drive outside and screamed to a halt. The noise of the tyres made me look towards it. A man climbed awkwardly out, straightened up and became Harvey Robbins. I grabbed Franks.

'Look, I should be so lucky. That's him.'

'That's who?'

'Robbins. The man you're enquiring about. Walking right into our hands.'

Interested now, he watched with me as Robbins unlocked the back of the car and pulled out a bag. Then as he bent to lock up, the lawyer must have sensed something. Swinging his head to the side he looked directly at us. I saw recognition in his eyes at once. He walked to the side of the car, swung the bag inside.

'He's leaving.' I got up. 'I'm going after him.'

Robbins was back in the car, roaring the motor. Franks said:

'You'll never catch him. Those things can travel.'

'How about a call to your radio boys,' I asked urgently.

'Sorry,' he refused. 'How can I justify it? The man hasn't done a thing.'

'I'll call you at your office later.'

I shouted that over my shoulder as I hurried from the bar. Maggie Murphy and her admirers watched curiously as I left. Outside, the red car was a dot heading back to Vale City. I jumped in the Chev and set off at a gallop after it. I could just manage to keep Robbins in sight by keeping the pedal flat on the floor. As I flashed by an intersection, I saw another car out of the corner of my eye. I hoped I hadn't seen the flashing lamp on the top, but soon the familiar wail from behind told me I was right.

It took them over a mile to catch me, but soon there they were. Alongside waving me over. I said a word I learned from a sailor one time and pulled into the side. A large and florid policeman came over, hands hooked in the shiny leather belt.

'Now, don't tell me you're gonna have a baby?'

'Look officer, I'm chasing somebody. Here. I'm a private investigator.'

I flashed my sticker and he inspected it gravely.

'This here is very pretty. But I don't see where it says you got any right to break every speed limit in the state.'

It was going to be one of those conversations. I gave up. In any case, with the ten minutes I'd already lost, Harvey Robbins would be practically into town by this time. Wearily, I went into my routine about working with the Vale police.

'Lieutenant Franks?' He liked that. 'Well, that's easy, mister. We'll just call headquarters and have him confirm.'

I explained that Franks was not in his office, but was back at the Tinklebell. That caused more discussion. Finally, they wrote down enough about me to fill a small biography, and threatened darkly about the consequences if the lieutenant did not back up my story. Then they went away.

There was no longer any point in hurrying, and I didn't do any speeding on the rest of the way into town. Although I felt it was hopeless, I spent some time rolling round the streets, watching out for Robbins' car. Having wasted about thirty minutes like that I gave up. Then I had to spend another ten minutes on the same kind of cruising, looking for somewhere to park. It was almost one-thirty, and I telephoned Franks' office to see if he'd arrived back, but he hadn't. They told me he was expected at two-fifteen, so I went into a diner and dawdled over a sandwich and a glass of milk. I made it last until ten after two, then got back to the car and drove over to headquarters. The lieutenant had left word at the desk, and I was shown straight to his office. He didn't look too happy to see me.

'Catch him?' he demanded.

'No. I got picked up by a patrol car for exceeding the limit. They'll be in touch with you, by the way.'

'H'm.'

His eyes went down to a piece of paper which lay in front of him, with some typed information on it.

'Got some stuff here about your boy. I guess he is a real lawyer?'

'I don't have any reason to doubt it,' I told him. 'Old Davis over in Los Angeles is not the type to be taken in by phoney credentials. Why do you ask?'

'Because all I know about friend Robbins is that he executed some legal documents while he was here. If he's a genuine lawyer, I guess that hardly constitutes grounds for indictment, huh?'

'No.'

Franks' attitude was worrying me. It wasn't much over an hour since we parted on good terms. Something must have happened in that time.

'Could I ask what your men found out about him?' I ventured.

'It's not much. He came here about five years ago. It could be a few months either way, that hasn't been checked in detail. He joined a local firm, Anderson and Warner. Very well known people, very respected. He did a lot of work for them, corporation stuff mostly. He also brought some business with him.'

He paused. Usually, that kind of pause is for dramatic effect, but I sensed that we were coming to the part Franks didn't like. I kept quiet.

'He was acting for the owners of a property in Monkton City. A company called A.B. Amusements. This company had rented out the property through Robbins, and he brought in a monthly commission on the deal.'

Another pause, and he looked at me this time.

'Oh good,' I said quietly. 'That is very, very good. That's the company I told you about. One of the owners was your boy Earnshaw. The fact that Robbins happened to be one lawyer out of hundreds in Los Angeles, who chanced to get the job of selling the place, well that's just normal routine. But this new stuff, the fact that he was also the man who acted for the same company in another town years before, that takes it out of the random class. Robbins is the key to this whole thing. I have to find him.'

'There's more. And this I'll tell you. All right, this A.B. Amusements outfit, I'll go along with you on that because it seems logical. But that doesn't mean there has to be something crooked about every deal he signed. Like I said, Anderson and Warner have been in business in Vale since the Indians, and I'm not going to stand for any mud being thrown around there.'

I didn't get it.

'Not following you too well,' I told him. 'I'm

only interested in Robbins. There's no suggestion about the firm he happened to work for while he was here. Any more than there is about the firm he works for today. What's all this leading up to, lieutenant?'

He drummed lightly on the table with well-kept fingers.

'Robbins brought in some other business when he came. He arranged the purchase of a roadhouse outside the town on behalf of one Margaret Murphy. We call it the Tinklebell.'

And that was the part he didn't like.

'Ah. A lady named Margaret Murphy. Or Maggie Murphy as she's known. Murphy and Robbins.'

'It doesn't have to mean anything,' he pointed out. 'Robbins must have closed dozens of deals for the firm while he was there. You want every one of those scrutinized?'

'No,' I agreed. 'But it was you singled out those two, not me. How did that happen?'

'Man who went over there to see Mr. Anderson. New feller, young, smart. He knows lawyers like other lawyers better when they bring some business with them. He figured if there was anything to learn about Robbins' past, a good lead might be found in any such business. So he asked, and Mr. Anderson remembered. Mr. Anderson is not a prominent local man for nothing.'

I lit an Old Favorite, wondering where we went next.

'As you say,' I said in a conciliatory tone, 'it doesn't have to mean anything at all. But you can see I'd be a fool not to glance it over.'

'I don't know what I see,' he replied irritably. 'I've known Maggie ever since she came to Vale. She's a wonderful person, runs a great place, made a lot of friends. Some of them very influential people around here. So she bought the place through this Robbins. So what?'

'So Robbins is definitely tied in with an old pornographic movie rap at least. He's quite possibly involved in murders, some of those not so old. Maggie Murphy arrived here at about the time of the Studio Six case back in Monkton. Just about the time somebody called Clara Jean Dollery disappeared from that same town.'

'I've heard nothing yet,' he returned doggedly.

I flicked ash rapidly into the bowl on his table.

'There's more. Judson, the man you call Earnshaw, said he was coming to Vale City. He did come, and he was murdered. Right in the forecourt of the Tinklebell, proprietor Maggie Murphy.'

'Wrong,' interrupted the detective briskly. 'The medical evidence was quite clear. The man had been killed somewhere else and dumped out at the Tinklebell. I told you that before.'

'You told me. Let's get back to Robbins. Is the Tinklebell a hotel?'

'You know it isn't.'

'Right. But when Robbins arrived he had some kind of bag with him. Why does a man carry a bag into a place which is just a bar? He was expecting to stay over.'

Some of the frown relaxed on the lieutenant's face.

'Oh come on,' he chuffed. 'I've heard of people moving the facts around to suit a particular theory, but that's kind of way out isn't it? I already said I go along with you on Robbins. I think you're right, I think he's in this mess somewhere. But just because a guy takes a bag into a bar, it doesn't mean he's going to sleep there. It means there's something in the bag he doesn't want out of his sight. Walk into any bar in town. You'll find plenty of people carrying all kinds of bags. You're really squeezing it, Preston.'

Put like that, I could follow his reasoning. The trouble was, I wasn't acting only on reason, but also on that other ingredient without which many investigations never get finished. Call it sixth sense, hunch, what you will, but I felt it. Franks leaned on his elbows, and said:

'Look Preston, I know you're all hipped up over this. You've done a lot of good work, dug out a lot of stuff. You can feel you're getting near the end and you want to hurry. I know the feeling, know it too well. But look at the facts. What have you got? You have a darned good prima facie case for having Robbins brought in. That man has a lot of questions to answer. Go ahead and get him. As for Maggie Murphy, well that's something else again. Believe me, and I know you think I'm prejudiced, if the lady is involved, I'll be the first one to apply for a warrant. But I wouldn't get one on all the hearsay and theory you've strung together. You said yourself, Robbins is the key. Get him. If he incriminates Maggie or anybody else in town, I'll bring 'em in. I don't care if it's the mayor himself, I'll do it. Meantime, what can you lose? She isn't going anywhere. That place is her living. She can't just wander away and leave it. She would have to go through all the procedures of selling it. And I would know. Believe me, if anything of that kind happens while you're digging out this Robbins, I'll slap a restraint order in very fast. Forget her for now. She'll be here if and when you ever happen to want her again. Even if it's only to apologize.'

He was absolutely right of course. I'd been letting myself get too excited. If I was right, and Maggie Murphy was the woman I was looking for, she couldn't afford to leave all that money tied up in the Tinklebell. And the woman I wanted wouldn't be the type to leave it either.

'You got me,' I agreed. 'Maybe I was

running when I ought to be walking. Can I ask you to put out a call on Robbins?'

'Glad to. And I'll talk to the people in Monkton City as well as the Los Angeles department. If they all agree, we ought to be able to make the territory fairly hot for Mr. Robbins. I suppose you'll go looking on your own?'

'I don't have anything else to do that's useful,' I nodded. 'Mind, I have to phone my client this afternoon. She may tell me to drop the whole thing. She's only looking for one lost little sister. She didn't say anything about bringing home a bagful of murderers, crooked lawyers and who knows what else.'

Franks got up and held out his hand.

'Good luck to you. Keep in touch, so you'll know if we pick up your boy.'

'Don't worry,' I assured him.

As I left the building, a big clock on the old-style cigar store opposite boomed three.

CHAPTER THIRTEEN

I got a pocketful of change and settled down beside a pay phone to call Little Falls. The operator was feeling the heat too, and I had to tell her where it was. Finally I got the Little Falls operator. When I told her the number I wanted, she said:

'Orange Patch? You want to speak to Miss Horan?'

'No, I happen to want somebody else. Her niece. Would you mind putting me through, please?'

'Well, I don't know if I ought,' she said doubtfully. 'The old lady ought to be getting her rest in the afternoon. She's a very sick woman you know. Can't it wait?'

Careful to keep irritation out of my voice, because I knew she'd cut me off if I didn't, I said:

'Look lady, this is not my idea. Mrs. Carter, that's the niece, asked me to call this afternoon. It's very important. It wouldn't surprise me if Miss Horan herself is also waiting to hear.'

'I see. Well, I guess it sounds alright. I mean, if it's some kind of emergency—'

She went on mumbling to herself while she rang the number.

'You see, there's nobody answering. I'm positive Miss Horan will be resting. Oh dear, oh dear. Oh, that you Miss Horan? Well, I certainly hope I didn't disturb you, ma'am. Yes, it's Ellie here. I have a man on the line, a Mr. Preston. Says he's supposed to call your niece. I told him you'd be resting. Yes ma'am. I surely will. Hold on please.'

Switching her voice back to me she said:

'There. I hope you're satisfied, Mr. Preston. I did wake up Miss Horan. She says Mrs.

195

Carter is not there and your office had a message for you not to call until late this evening. Mrs. Carter will be home then.'

'I see. And that's all?'

'That's all? I should think that's enough for one afternoon. Waking up an invalid indeed. Well, is there any message?'

I didn't feel I could cope with very much more of Ellie.

'Thank you, yes. Please tell Miss Horan I'll call about eight tonight if that's all right.'

There was more mumbling at the other end.

'Are you there? Miss Horan says nine thirty would be better.'

'Thank you. I'll do that.'

I put the phone down thankfully. Then I thumbed through the Vale directory. There were only three M. Murphys in the book, and only one of those was Miss. The listed address was a place on South Street. I noted the number and went out on to the street. A passerby told me that South Street was seven blocks east of where we were. As I drove along I was remembering what Franks had said, wondering whether he wasn't right, and I was merely chasing my tail.

South Street was a quiet residential neighborhood, small neat houses laying well back from the road. The number I wanted looked no different from the rest. Well, what did I expect? Barricades and machine guns? I felt quick disappointment too, when there was no sign of Robbins' car out front. I parked outside, and sat looking at the house for a moment. There wasn't much to see, just walls and windows. Climbing out, I walked up the narrow stone path to the front door. There was no bell, just an old-fashioned brass knocker, which clumped heavily against the door. After a few moments I heard someone behind the door. Then it opened. Maggie Murphy looked as good in the sunlight as she had in the bar. She looked surprised.

'Well, well. You're Lieutenant Franks' friend aren't you? Mr.—'

'Preston.'

'Yes. What can I do for you, Mr. Preston?'

'I'd like to talk to you for a minute if it's possible.'

She didn't seem very enthusiastic.

'It would have to be important for you to come to my house,' she said brusquely. 'Couldn't it wait until I'm at work tonight?'

'It's important to me, Miss Murphy. I'd prefer now if you don't mind.'

'Oh very well. You'd better come in.'

The door closed behind me.

'In here.'

She led me into a large comfortable room, and sat herself down.

'I hope this won't take too long, Mr. Preston. I usually try to relax for a couple of hours in the afternoon. I work a long evening, you know.'

'Thank you for giving me the time. May I?'

I pointed to a chair.

'Yes, of course. Cigaret?'

She held out a sandalwood box, and sun flashed quickly from the giant emerald on her hand. I held out flame and she inhaled deeply, throwing back her head.

'Ready when you are.'

'Miss Murphy, I'm a private investigator, working with the police on some enquiries. I'm very interested in someone you know, a man named Harvey Robbins.'

'Harvey? What's he supposed to have done?'

It was a promising start. At least she hadn't said she didn't know him.

'Maybe nothing,' I answered her. 'I'm just filling in some details. I believe you came to Vale City about five years ago?'

'As long as that? Well, I hadn't realized how the time goes. Yes, yes, I suppose it was about that.'

Better and better. She was very relaxed and composed.

'May I ask how you came to know him?'

She looked at me calmly.

'What is this supposed to be, Mr. Preston? I thought you wanted to ask about Harvey?'

'I do,' I assured her. 'But you see, Harvey and you would appear to have arrived in Vale City at about the same time.'

'And?'

'And I wondered whether you might have arrived together.'

'Look here, I'm damned if I'm going to be cross-examined by you. Whatever Harvey may have done is his concern, not mine.'

For some reason she was less at ease than before. She got up from the chair irritably.

'I think you'd better go. You haven't any right to be here. You get into the house under false pretenses. I may take this up with Lieutenant Franks. He and his wife are my friends, you know.'

Her voice was snappish and peremptory, but I thought I detected something there that had more to do with fear than genuine outrage. I stood up, as if about to leave.

'Oh by the way,' and I watched her face, 'I also want information about a woman who came here five years ago. Her name was Clara Jean Dollery. You didn't happen to run into her back then?'

'No. Now go.'

It could have been my imagination, but I thought her eyes showed alarm when I mentioned the name.

'It doesn't matter,' I shrugged. 'I have a man meeting me this afternoon who knew her from the old Studio Six days. He remembers her very well.'

'Harvey.'

She said it in a low hiss, and there was a movement in the doorway behind me. I turned

199

to see Robbins standing there, his face contorted with anxious fear. But the blue automatic in his hand was steady enough.

'I told you,' he blurted out. 'I warned you this man—'

'Shut up. If he moves, kill him.'

'Well well, Harvey,' I greeted. 'I didn't have you figured for a killer. I thought you were more or less an innocent bystander.'

'Listen, Preston,' he began, but Maggie cut him off.

'Quiet. You, take off your coat.'

I took off the coat. She stared at the .38 tucked under my arm. Then she came close, pulling the gun out of its holster. That was my chance. I grabbed her extended arm and began to pull her between me and Harvey. I say began, because she at once brought up her pointed shoe into my groin and I sank to my knees, clutching at myself.

'What do you think this is, amateur night?' she laughed.

'Honey, I think—'

'Nobody cares what you think, Harvey. Just do as I say, and this will work out all right.'

She stood, holding the .38 and looking down at me.

'I like to know who I'm killing,' she remarked almost casually. 'Tell me why you started all this. What did I ever do to you?'

I told her to go somewhere. She swung the gun lightly across my face. My head jerked as

200

the cheek split and blood ran down.

'For God's sake,' protested Harvey.

She swung round fiercely at him.

'For God's sake,' she mimicked. 'You don't like this do you? You don't like the hard parts, the dirty work. But you take the money.'

Robbins went white.

'Listen, I do what I do because I love you. But I'll be no party to murder.'

'Won't you really? What do you suggest we do with this character? Drive him down to police headquarters? We don't have any choice.'

His head bobbed up and down eagerly.

'But we do, we do. We're ready to leave, right now. Everything has been taken care of. Once we get clear of this city, nobody'll ever find us. All we need is a few hours start. There doesn't have to be any killing. And besides, I— I couldn't do it.'

Maggie snorted impatiently.

'Ah. Nobody expects you to do it. But there may be something in what you say. Pity to butcher a good-looking hunk of man when there's no necessity. Well, what do you say, Preston?'

About to give her the answer she deserved, I remembered the split cheek in time and changed my mind.

'You won't get very far before you're picked up. If you knock me off, you'll just be giving the law an open and shut case. They won't

201

even have to bother about proving any of the old stuff.'

'Ah.'

She pursed her lips and nodded.

'That's the part that makes sense. Yes, that's very good. All right, Harvey, get a rope from the garage.'

When he'd gone, she stepped back so she'd have plenty of time for a clear shot in case I got brave. I didn't.

'Tell me one thing,' I muttered. 'I've been to a lot of trouble to find it out, and you're almost certainly my last chance.'

She grinned, and winked at me.

'You sure have your nerve, brother Preston. You and I, we would've been great together. What do you want to know?'

'In the old days, back in Monkton City, there was a girl.'

'A girl? Man, we had those in carloads.'

'This was a particular one I'm interested in. Her name was Anthea Horan. Does it ring any bells?'

Her face softened briefly.

'What about her?' she demanded. 'Maybe I do recall something.'

'She's the one I'm looking for,' I explained. 'Her sister hired me to look for her.'

Her eyes widened, and she spoke almost before she realized it.

'Cornelia? She—'

Then she stopped, and her mouth

tightened. And now I had it. I already knew there wasn't any Maggie Murphy, nor Mrs. James Earnshaw, but I'd never doubted there was such a person as Clara Jean Dollery. And now, it seemed I was wrong. There never was anybody else but Anthea. And I'd never suspected it.

'So you're Anthea,' I said softly. 'I don't know how Cornelia will take it when I tell her.'

'Who cares how she takes it?' she snarled. 'Goody Two Shoes had nothing on my dear sister. I thought she went off somewhere with a bible-thumper?'

'Africa. He died, and she came home. Wanted to find you.

'Huh,' she sneered. 'I never had any use for her when we were girls. I can just imagine what she's like now. So, finally, I have a really good reason for keeping you alive, don't I? You go and tell my sweet little sister all about me. Leave nothing out, please.'

'Including how you killed Judson? And Stone?'

She shrugged.

'It doesn't matter. They had plenty from me, both of them. This is a hard world for a girl trying to make her way, Preston. Every now and then you have to be as tough as the next. Tougher.'

'I could understand Judson. He probably tried to shake you down. But why Stone suddenly? He'd been around a long time.'

'Bob Stone was a fool. He'd still be alive if he hadn't tried to double-cross me. He sold the Red Pig without me knowing it. He was going to take the money and go. He should have known better than that.'

'Anthea.'

Harvey stood in the doorway, a rope hanging from his hand. He was staring at her and shaking his head in a bemused fashion.

'Anthea, you told me you knew nothing about it. You swore—'

'Well, now you know. Get on and tie him up.'

He didn't move, and now her face changed.

'You get this, Harvey. I'm leaving here, with or without you. If I leave you, you'll be dead. I haven't come this far just to have everything balled up because you're too squeamish to face realities. You, Preston, get in that chair.'

I moved. This woman had killed before, and I hadn't any doubt she'd do it again if she had to. Harvey began roping me to the chair, and the way he was doing it told me I'd be a long time getting free.

'That'll do. Let's go.'

She picked up a grip from behind a bureau.

'So long, Preston. And don't get the idea this is any of your doing. I've been planning to move on for months. You hurried things along, that's all.'

I stared at her silently. I was trying to work out what this disappearing act was going to be.

For this woman to take the risk of leaving me alive it had to be foolproof. Somehow, I didn't feel I was ever going to see Anthea again, and neither was anyone else. She gave me a mocking smile, and nodded at Harvey, still busy behind me. The force of the blow was enough to topple both me and the chair forward. I got a mouthful of carpet just before the darkness closed over me.

CHAPTER FOURTEEN

Something sharp and unpleasant hit my nostrils, and I jerked my head away from it.

'He's coming round,' said a voice.

Again the bitter smell, and again I pulled away, opening my eyes.

'What the hell are you doing?' I grumbled.

I was lying on a canvas covered stretcher, in a plain, square room. There was a man leaning over me, a man in a white coat, with a stethoscope dangling from his neck. It was daylight.

'How're you feeling, Preston?'

Franks' anxious voice came from a different direction. I made the mistake of turning my head towards him, and something thumped the top of my spinal column.

'Hi, Lieutenant,' I grumbled. 'What happened?'

'I was hoping you'd tell us that. Is he O.K. doc?'

The doctor nodded, standing up.

'Nothing wrong with him. He'll have a sore head for a while, but that's all. I have some patients to see to, Lieutenant.'

'Sure, of course. Many thanks.'

When we were alone in the room, Franks said:

'If you're looking for your cigarets, they're here.'

'Thanks.'

The smoke tasted like rusty nails in my throat.

'You feel up to telling me what happened at the house?'

'Not much to it. I called on your friend Miss Murphy. Harvey Robbins was there. They showed me a gun, tied me up, and banged me over the head.'

'Just like that? Why?'

I told him about our conversation, what there had been of it. He listened, made notes on a small pad he'd taken from his pocket.

'Anthea Horan? The dame you were looking for, after all these years? Kind of hard to credit isn't it?'

'She ought to know her own name,' I told him. 'Besides, I'm through with it now. I was hired to find Anthea, I found her. Now I collect my fee and bow out. What happens to Anthea is your problem.'

He looked at me strangely.

'Not any more,' he denied. 'Aren't you curious about how we found you?'

'I figure you'll tell me if I wait long enough.'

'She's dead, Preston. A few miles outside of town, the state patrol found the car. All smashed up, and burned out in the rocks. It was when investigating officers came to the house to get an idea of her next of kin, they found you.'

'Wow,' I muttered. 'And Harvey? Did he survive it?'

An odd look came over Franks' face.

'Oh yes, he survived. In fact it would seem we all underestimated Mr. Robbins. Particularly you. You had him figured for a harmless character who picked the wrong woman, right?'

'Something like that,' I agreed.

'Well, Robbins had a little something extra up his sleeve. Maggie was murdered, no doubt of it. It was a crude attempt to make it look like a crash blaze. But the skid marks and so forth all indicate the car wasn't travelling fast enough for that much damage. It was a plant. And Harvey got away.'

I nodded, thinking.

'Doesn't sound like that woman, to get caught easily. I wouldn't have thought Robbins could do it. I'd have understood it better the other way around. Maybe he shot her first, or strangled her?'

'We'll never know. I never saw such a mess as that body. Anyhow, don't worry about Harvey. We have him already.'

'Good. In fact, congratulations. Pretty fast work.'

Franks nodded slowly, and didn't seem too impressed by the compliment.

'No congratulations due. He's dead as well.'

'But I thought you said he got away?' I queried.

'From the crash, yes. But he got too smart for himself. After he set fire to the car, he must have figured it was too risky just thumbing a ride on the same road. So he headed for Highway 66. That's a mile or two cross country from the crash. Some tricky rocks to get over, and maybe he wasn't in condition or something. Anyway, he fell down a cliff and broke his neck. Only a few hundred yards from the car. And that winds it up.'

'H'm.' I smoked and studied the ceiling. 'Did you find the money?'

He looked at me narrowly.

'Who said there was any money to find?' he demanded.

'Oh come on, Lieutenant. Those lovebirds had planned all this. There had to be money.'

'Yes,' he assented. 'There was. There was a bag not far from the body with several thousand dollars in it. And that about wraps the whole thing up.'

Pity, I reflected. I was hoping the money would be missing, so I could dream up some alternative to Franks' reasoning. It just didn't sit right with me. Any dame as smart as Anthea Horan had been all these years didn't have any right to be beaten in the end by a weak sister like Harvey Robbins. Still, I recalled, a lot of great figures have been brought down by insignificant people. And I would hardly classify Anthea as a great figure. Nevertheless, I felt cheated, somehow.

'Going to be busy,' stated the policeman, getting up. 'This little matter is going to close a lot of files in a lot of places. But there's a heap of paper to be got through, before it's done. Drop around tomorrow can you, and we'll get some of it down?'

'Sure. Tomorrow.'

At the door, he turned and grinned.

'And, by the way, thanks. I don't know how you got all this started but things certainly moved once you did.'

'It's the time limit,' I explained. 'My client only gave me till today. After that, no pay envelope.'

He flipped a hand, and went out. Unless my watch had been damaged by the fall, it was now six o'clock. I was due to call Cornelia Carter at nine thirty, and I wasn't looking forward to it with any relish. Considering what I had found out about Anthea, which was bad enough, and then thinking of the end of the story, it was one telephone call I could live without. The more I thought about it, the less I liked the prospect. From what I knew of the set-up at Orange Patch, there was this elderly, sick aunt, and the mousey, spinsterish Cornelia, widow or not. A fairly close community, as I visualized it, probably confined to a very narrow domestic routine. Not the kind of household where shocks would be quickly absorbed or brushed off. And it was the way of delivering the shock too, that made me uneasy. A few sentences over the phone, from a couple of hundred miles away. And from a total stranger. That is no way to learn this kind of news. I lay there fretting about it for a while, then I decided what I had to do. Getting up, I located my jacket hung neatly in a closet, and slipped it on. My shoes were under the stretcher.

Outside I found a public phone in the lobby, and dialled the local airport. There was one local trip to Fresno at seven forty, which gave me plenty of time. I called police headquarters and left a message for Franks to say I'd be back in Monkton City the next day. Then I went out into the evening sun and called a cab. The airfield was twenty minutes outside of town, and the cabbie filled the journey with a dramatic and wholly inaccurate description of what had happened to Robbins and Maggie Murphy. As he explained confidentially, he was telling me a lot more than I'd hear on

210

television or radio, because he had this buddy with a direct in at headquarters.

'Mark you,' he said knowingly, 'this Preston, this private eye character, there's a lot we don't know about him yet. Way I hear it, he's probably in this up to his neck.'

'That so?' I replied.

'You bet,' he confirmed. 'I mean, this guy was supposed to be here working on some case, and he finds out all this? Or so they'd have us believe. Way I see it, you don't tip over a mess of vegetables that size by accident.'

'Doesn't seem likely,' I agreed.

'You bet it ain't. Well, here we are. You going far, buddy?'

'Just over to Fresno.'

'Fresno,' he sighed. 'Takes me back. I knew a girl over there one time. Sure takes me back.'

I didn't ask him about the girl, in case she turned out to be one of the Horan sisters, or worse still, Aunt Emma. I couldn't stomach any more complications. He gave me a cheery grin as he drove away to continue spreading slander about me all over Vale City.

Going into the small terminal building, I had a couple of cool beers while waiting for the plane. It arrived bang on schedule and I got a seat up near the rear. The hostess eyed me glassily, the way they do healthy males who want to sit at the back of the aircraft. She didn't want to spend the whole trip sidestepping. To reassure her, I said:

'If I should chance to fall asleep, you will be sure I get off at Fresno, won't you? I'm an invalid, you see, and any kind of motion rocks me off.'

At once, the suspicion dissolved, and she insisted on fetching me a blanket. What with the blanket and the drone of the engines, I really did conk off, to be woken by a gentle shake.

'Fresno in five minutes,' she whispered.

I'd overdone the invalid thing. She insisted on helping me down the steep steps at the airfield, and for two pins she'd have had me in a wheelchair. She was a pretty little thing, all button nose and shining curls tucked under the cute cap. I made a note to put the invalid routine to better use one of these days, and climbed into a cab for Fresno. I told the driver I wanted to rent a car, and he took me to an all night garage that could help. The man there was not enthusiastic.

'Stranger in town?' he queried. 'And it's just for one night, huh?'

I imagine in the car rent business, if you don't ask the right questions, you can wind up minus a lot of cars. I showed him my sticker.

'It's good anywhere in the state,' I assured him. 'All you have to do is make a note of the license number.'

He cheered up a little at that.

'Yeah. Yeah, this looks O.K. Mind if I write it down?'

'Help yourself.'

He scribbled quickly, and returned the billfold to me.

'Now, let's see,' he scratched his head, 'Don't have a lot left to offer you, Mr. Preston. Weekend we get quite a lot of calls.'

'Anything on wheels, and not too fancy. Place I'm going is a farm, and I don't know what the roads will be like.'

'Got the very thing,' he announced. 'Four year old Chev. Little chipped, here and there, but good springs. Just the thing for those farm roads.'

'Sounds ideal,' I told him. 'Drive a Chev myself, back home.'

I passed over some bills, and asked him the way to Little Falls.

'Turn east three blocks along, and that is the county road clear through to Little Falls. Know it well. Which particular farm you interested in?'

'Orange Patch. You know it?'

'I would hope so. Like everybody else for miles. That's Aunt Emma's place. The old lady is kind of an institution hereabouts. Real old pioneer stock. One of the last of the frontier women, who really did fight Indians. Them redskins only knew it, they never had a chance with Aunt Emma. You kin of hers?'

'No, I'm just doing a little business for her.'

'Business, yes, she's—good at that. The way she's built that place these past fifty years. Got

213

thirty people working the whole year round, you know. Near a hundred and fifty at picking time. Orange Patch,' he said amusedly. 'Sounds like a little dirt farm, don't it? Queer name for a place worth more than a million dollars. Now, here's how you get there. Once you go through Little Falls—'

And he went off into a closely detailed route which practically took me to the front door of the farm. I thanked him, and he shook hands heartily, before shepherding me into the car and waving me out.

His directions were so explicit I could have found my way in the dark. As it was the dying sun was giving off plenty of light when I reached the small turn-off marked 'Orange Patch'. I drove slowly along the winding, bumpy road, between neat rows of trees that seemed to stretch forever on both sides. It was nine forty when I came in sight of the house, a low, rambling, white-painted structure. You could see quite clearly where extra building had been tacked on and around the original cabin. There were lights on, and I revved the engine noisily, so people would know they had a visitor. As I got out of the car, a man scrunched heavily towards me.

'Evening,' he greeted. 'You visiting?'

'Yes, I'm calling to see Mrs. Carter,' I told him.

'I'm Troughton, foreman here. Mrs. Carter know you're coming?'

'No, I'm supposed to telephone, but I preferred to come personally.'

'H'm.'

He hooked his thumbs in a thick leather belt, and thought.

'Don't get too many visitors, specially at this hour,' he grunted.

'I would have come earlier, but I understood Mrs. Carter wouldn't be back home till late.'

'H'm. That's true. That's true enough. She just got back an hour ago. Tell you what, you understand, that there house only just has the two ladies in it. Might get 'em all flustered if visitors turn up unexpected. Why don't you just have yourself a smoke a minute, while I go tell 'em you're here?'

'Fine.' I agreed. 'Oh, and the name is Preston.'

He acknowledged that with a nod, and turned to tramp up to the farmhouse. He knocked at a door, which opened, and he went in. After a couple of minutes he came back out, beckoning to me.

'You're to go right in.'

I left the keys in the dash. It seemed to me there wouldn't be too many car thieves around Orange Patch. At the doorway, the foreman pointed inside.

'In there, second door on your right.'

'Thanks.'

I went in the hallway and tapped at the

215

second door.

'Come in.'

I opened it, and went into a large comfortable room, the kind with deep easy chairs with lace covers on the back. Facing me, an old lady sat in a wheelchair, her lined, tanned face creased into a smile.

'You're Mr. Preston, aren't you? Call me Aunt Emma. Everybody does.'

I shook a surprisingly firm hand.

'Sit down, young man. You don't smoke a pipe, do you?'

'I'm afraid not. Just cigarets.'

She had sounded hopeful, looked slightly disappointed.

'Pipe is better. Still, go ahead with the cigaret. I like a man to smoke. And we don't get all that many callers these days.'

Dutifully, I fished out my Old Favorites and lit one. She watched with approval, nodding slightly as I leaned back.

'Good, good. You're wondering where Cornelia is, naturally. Well, as soon as she heard you were here, she rushed upstairs to change her clothes. Said something about her hair, too. Women don't change much, do they? Still, I was gratified. Didn't think Cornelia had it in her any more. Never did, much, even as a girl.'

That was something about which I certainly was not going to have any opinion, so I was glad to be able to concentrate on the smoke.

'I'm dying to ask you about Anthea, and what you've been doing,' she prattled on, 'but it wouldn't be fair to Cornelia.'

'Well,' I agreed, 'if you wouldn't mind?'

'No. 'Twouldn't be fair. After all, she's the one hiring you.'

I was wondering whether Aunt Emma should be present at all when I told my story. She was obviously an invalid and Cornelia had told me she had to be looked after. For all her vigorous conversation, I had no way of knowing whether she would be able to withstand any kind of shock, and my history of the late unlamented Anthea would certainly qualify in the shock category.

'Don't keep any liquor in the house, I'm afraid,' she apologised.

'That's perfectly all right, ma'am, I'm very comfortable.'

There was the sound of someone coming downstairs. I watched the door, stood as it opened. Cornelia, or Mrs. Erasmus Carter Jnr., had not improved since I last saw her. She was as uncertain as I remembered, hands fluttering, hair untidy. But now I realized why I'd thought Maggie Murphy looked familiar at first sight. There was an undoubted resemblance. The difference was that Maggie had emphasized all her good features, played down any bad. The unfortunate Cornelia just hadn't the first notion of how to present the article, as the ad boys say.

217

'Why, Mr. Preston,' she fluted. 'I thought you were to telephone.'

She began darting helplessly about. Aunt Emma said:

'Cornelia, go and sit down. It's very hard on my eyes, trying to keep you in view.'

At once, she did as instructed, rushing to a chair and sinking into it. Thankfully, I sat down.

'The point is, Mrs. Carter. There's such a lot to tell, I really felt I ought to come myself.'

'Still,' she said doubtfully, 'it's a very expensive journey.'

So that was it.

'Please don't worry about it,' I begged. 'This is on my own time.'

'Nonsense,' snapped Aunt Emma. 'We're not poor people, Mr. Preston. Please get on with the story.'

I looked at her doubtfully.

'The fact is Aunt Emma,' I began slowly, 'some of this doesn't make very good listening. You being not well, I wonder whether—'

She interrupted with a short laugh.

'So that's it? You think I might die of shock? Well, let me tell you, I have more things wrong with me than you could imagine. But the heart isn't one, thank heaven. The doctors tell me I have a heart like an ox.'

I turned to Cornelia for confirmation. She nodded brightly.

'Oh it's quite true. Aunt Emma is tough

enough to be a—a—'

Her voice tailed away. She'd forgotten the rest.

'A drill sergeant, that's what,' finished the formidable old lady.

And that seemed to settle it.

'Anthea is dead, isn't she?' asked Cornelia softly.

'Yes,' I replied simply. 'I'm sorry.'

'There couldn't be any doubt?' and the toughness had left Aunt Emma's voice.

When I shook my head, she said, in a faraway voice:

'Such a pretty little thing, she was. Such a lovely face.'

'Were you able to get any of the details?' queried Cornelia, in a low voice.

'I have a great deal to tell you, and I'm sorry to have to say most of it isn't very nice.'

Aunt Emma folded her hands in her lap.

'I've waited many years to learn all this, Mr. Preston. Please.'

I started to talk. It wasn't a pretty story, and there wasn't any way I could make it prettier. At first there were oohs and ahs from my little audience, but they relapsed gradually into stony silence, each of them staring at the floor. It took some time to tell. And I found need of another cigaret halfway through. When I finished finally, there was silence. Neither of them moved or spoke.

'I'm sorry,' I said apologetically. 'I wish I

could have told you some other way.'

'Such a pretty little thing,' said the old lady abstractedly.

Cornelia dug around for a handkerchief, and began to sniffle quietly. I wished I'd settled for the telephone call after all. Aunt Emma propelled herself across to where her niece was sitting, and put an arm round her with surprising gentleness.

'You see, Mr. Preston,' she told me, 'we're all alone now, she and I. Although we've been apart all these years, I always knew I had two nieces somewhere, and Cornelia always knew she had a sister. Now here, tonight, we suddenly find we're alone. You must forgive us, after all the trouble you've been to.'

I fumbled with my feet. Cornelia looked up suddenly.

'Mr. Preston, I had many doubts about coming to you. in the first place. But I think you've done wonders. I really do.'

'Hear hear,' said Aunt Emma.

I got up, I'd done what I had to do, and there wasn't any point in remaining any longer.

'Will it all come out?' asked Cornelia tremulously.

'I'm afraid it will,' I nodded. 'The police know most of it already.'

'And they'll come here? All those awful people, and our pictures in the paper and everything?'

I looked at them, each in turn.

'I hope not,' I said softly. 'They won't get your names from me.'

Cornelia nodded thankfully.

'Well, ladies, it's pretty late,' I muttered, 'I ought to think about getting back.'

Cornelia began to weep again. Aunt Emma held out her hand.

'I'd ask you to stay, Mr. Preston, but in the circumstances—'

'Don't bother to see me out. I'm sorry to be the bearer of such news.'

I left them there, alone with their thoughts, and each other. I'd been lying about that drink. I realized I could do with one. Outside, I found I'd been too optimistic about the car-snatchers at Orange Patch. The Chev was gone. Then Troughton loomed up out of the darkness.

'Sorry about the car,' he greeted. 'I had to get a big truck through while you were inside. I took your car around the back of the house to the garage. Hope you don't mind.'

'No, certainly not. Round that way?'

'Yup. You can't miss it. 'Bout a hundred yards.'

I thanked him and walked off. It was dark at the back of the house, but I could just make out the familiar shape. Climbing inside, I switched on the motor and snapped down the headlight switch. I eased off the brake and rolled slowly forward, turning at the side of the house, the big headlights cutting through the

221

night. I looked again at what I thought I saw, braked sharply, and switched off. There in front of me, twenty feet away, was Harvey Robbins' car. I stared at it stupidly. I'd made a mistake of course. Plenty of red sports cars around. I'd had a tough day, not to mention getting banged over the head. Everybody's entitled to foul up once in a while. Getting out, I walked over to get a close look. There was no mistake.

Turning, I shambled back to the Chev, got in and slumped behind the wheel—I had to think, but my mind was only a confused whirl. I sat there, staring out, and trying to straighten my thoughts.

CHAPTER FIFTEEN

When I got back to the house, the front door was closed. I tapped and Cornelia opened it.

'Oh, Mr. Preston, did you forget something?'

'Yes. Could I come in?'

'Well—yes. Yes of course. Come on.'

She closed the door, and we went back into the same room.

'Aunt Emma's gone to bed, I'm afraid. Just excuse me, while I go and tell her, otherwise she'll be worrying about who it was at the door.'

I sat down wearily. Then I noticed a bottle of rye which had appeared on a sideboard. There was only one glass, but I wasn't in the mood to be polite. I splashed out about four fingers and drank deeply. It was good. Before sitting again, I helped myself to some more of the same. Cornelia came back in, and her mouth went thin at the sight of the glass.

'Well, I must say, people usually wait till they're asked.'

She left the door primly open, in case the drunken private eye thought he was going to get fresh with the widow of that great missionary, Erasmus Carter Jnr. I raised my glass.

'To you honey. You're great. By the way, Aunt Emma doesn't know about the bottle, so it has to be yours. Why don't you get yourself another glass?'

'H'mph.'

She snorted, turned on her heels and went out. When she came back, she was toting an extra glass.

'It's just a small habit I acquired over in Africa. Not that I have to explain myself to you.'

'That you don't,' I agreed morosely. 'Anyway, I doubt whether you could explain yourself to you.'

The way she sank the first ration of rye indicated she was no stranger to the art.

'I don't understand you,' she snapped

irritably. 'Fifteen minutes ago you were as nice as can be. Now you've turned all peculiar.'

'Time,' I assured her solemnly. 'Time wounds all heels. I believe I'll take some more of the same.'

I grabbed up the bottle before she could reach it, and poured myself a good helping. I held it out to her, and after a momentary hesitation, she extended her glass.

'Good. Good. You and I ought to drink together, Cornelia. Because, and we have to face this, you are a very remarkable woman. And I, for my humble part, am a very remarkable chump.'

She drummed her fingernails against the side of the glass.

'Mr. Preston, if you came back for a drink, you've had one. Will you please go now?'

I laughed, and the amusement was genuine.

'How long can you go on this way?' I demanded. 'Angel face, the bets are laid, the game, as they persist in saying, is over.'

'Well,' she said hesitantly, 'If I must humor you, I must.'

She parked herself primly on the edge of a chair, darting anxious glances towards the open door.

'Cornelia,' I entreated, 'let's be frank, you and I. I've seen Harvey's car.'

'I don't know what you're talking about,' she pouted.

'Aw, come on. You remember old Harve.

You just got through killing him this afternoon.'

She tipped down some more of the rye, and stared at me.

'You know,' I confided, 'I've been admiring the wrong girl. There I was, thinking how smart Anthea was. What an operator, Anthea, Clara Jean, Maggie Murphy, Mrs. Earnshaw. I mean, you put up the circumstances, Anthea had a name for them, and a character to go with it.'

'She was dreadful. Quite totally dreadful,' bit Cornelia.

I waved a deprecatory arm.

'Tut tut,' I tut-tutted, 'shame on you. She never existed. At least, not on that Monkton, Vale City, L.A. trail. That wasn't her at all. That was you, honey. Sweet little old missionary Mrs. Cornelia.'

'You're drunk. If you don't go now I'll—'

'You'll what? Call the police? Please don't trouble yourself. I'm about to call them anyway. Believe me, this is a personal matter with me. Because I've been taken to the cleaners many times in my unhealthy life, but never so beautifully, never so completely.'

I waited to see if she had anything to offer, but no. At least she'd stopped glancing at the door.

'I thought I was pretty good, following up that old trail. That dusty, years old, Anthea trail. Pretty good. I should have realized

225

nobody is that good. But being me, I gave myself the credit. And you anticipated that I would, you saw it all. Like they say in bad movies, I raises me glass to you, Cornelia.'

She regarded me coolly. None of the birdie glances now, just the level stare of a self-composed woman.

'Just to humour you, before I bring the sheriff, what is all that supposed to mean?'

'Ah,' I wagged a finger. 'Ah. I've been worrying about that. Out there in the car, that's what was worrying me. What does it all mean? And it wasn't till I came here to Orange Patch, that I had the answer. Even when I had it, I didn't recognize it, not till I saw poor old Harve's car.'

I reached for the bottle, but this time she was too quick for me, and I watched regretfully, as it disappeared from reach.

'Man in Fresno,' I confided. 'He told me. But I didn't know what he was telling me, till I saw Harvey's car.'

She laughed then. Not the dried cackle of Mrs. Erasmus Carter Jnr., but the deep chuckle I would have expected from Maggie Murphy.

'This man in Fresno,' she said, humoring me. 'Tell me about his wonderful revelations.'

'Revelations,' I mused. 'They weren't really revelations. Just common everyday knowledge. But in this business you have to learn that what is everyday knowledge in one place, is the key

226

to momentous events in others. Did I say that, momentous events?'

'You did. Go on, Preston.'

We were making progress. I was no longer 'Mr.' Preston.

'Let's take two girls. One good, one bad. Oh, one very, very bad indeed. These girls have an aunt. One day, it turns out that Auntie is worth a lot of money. In fact, dear old Auntie is worth more than a million dollars. The bad niece gets to hear about this, and she wants in. In fact, she practically insists on it. So she turns up from nowhere, complete with her I-love-you-Auntie kit and a sad past. You know, that's very good.'

'What's very good?'

'The sad past. Because believe me angel, your past is as sad as a past can get. But I mustn't wander. Now the only obstacle remaining is to guarantee inheritance. So the bad niece hires a nice, simple-minded, honest kind of character. A me kind of character. Somebody who can be relied on to pick up a lead, if it's dangled in front of him long enough. Someone who will follow that lead, and then with luck, pick up the next one, if it's in plain enough sight. Lady, I have been played for a sucker by experts, but you have created a new class.'

She laughed again, and drained her glass. She then proceeded to replenish it, but I was not included in the offer.

227

'Oh, Preston, you play yourself down. I didn't need a chump. A chump I would have got cheaper. No, I needed somebody with some brains, and a touch of the old moxie to go with it. That's why you got the job. Don't be so modest.'

I surveyed my empty glass morosely, but it didn't tug at anybody's heart-strings but mine. I turned sour.

'You set me on this like a hound dog, to prove that Anthea was dead. All right, I've proved it. Or more accurately, I've proved that your trail proves that Anthea is dead. That leaves you free to inherit Aunt Emma's money. As far as it goes.'

I paused, in what I hoped was a significant fashion. Cornelia looked at me oddly.

'How do you mean, as far as it goes? As far as it goes, that's the end of the line.'

'No, no,' I denied. 'I mean that burned-up girl in the car. Someone is going to worry about her, sooner or later. That could upset things.'

'A hitch-hiker,' she sneered. 'There isn't enough left of her to make a sandwich. And, she was wearing my ring. Remember?'

She tapped at her hand, where Maggie Murphy had sported the king-size emerald.

'You may well have a point there,' I agreed. 'But all it will prove ultimately is that Maggie etc, etc. is dead. It doesn't take account of the real Anthea. And that's where you slipped up,

228

beautiful. Because, at the end of it all, the real Anthea, your dear sweet sister, can just walk in from nowhere, and claim her share. Or maybe claim it all, for all I know, if there's an old will.'

She shook her head regretfully, and from inside her dress produced a small nickel-plated automatic. It was a tiny gun, a woman's gun. But it would kill, properly used. And I knew enough of the woman opposite to know it would be properly used.

'Sometimes,' she remarked conversationally, 'you can be so smart. And sometimes you talk as though you just got off the banana boat. You haven't fathomed this at all, have you? Not really.'

'Oh, I don't know,' I disclaimed modestly, trying to ignore the gun. 'I don't think I've done too badly.'

'Fool. If we'd only met sooner, we'd be running this country today, you and I. I'm afraid it's too late now, Preston.'

She raised the gun, and I pretended not to be afraid. I don't think I was being very good at it.

'You can't kill me, Cornelia. This is in your new character. Whatever the others did, Anthea, Maggie and the rest, that's all buried, along with them. But Cornelia doesn't have this kind of background. Kill me, and you spoil everything.'

Slowly, she shook her head.

'Uh uh,' she negatived. 'It's completely in

229

character. Think about it. Think about Cornelia, as she's known hereabouts. There's no connection with these other things. There she is, the sorrowing widow of a missionary. In comes a drunken private eye, and tries to rape her. And by the way, the contents of your stomach will show you could have been drunk.'

She looked at me expectantly, but I didn't want to think about the contents of my stomach. In particular, I didn't want to think about those contents being splashed all over Aunt Emma's nice carpet. The gun came up level. Desperately I held up a hand.

'Wait,' I shouted. 'You're forgetting the real Anthea.'

'No,' she returned composedly. 'No, I'm not. You still haven't understood it, chump. I use your own word, chump. There isn't any real Anthea, not any more. That's what started all this. She died, right here on the farm, all those years back. It was Joe and me. We didn't mean to kill her, but it was a fun party, and she wouldn't join in.'

'Ah,' I said slowly. 'So Joe took off, and you had to invent this Carter, the man you were going to marry, so you could stay behind and say that Anthea left with Joe.'

'Finally, at last, you have the picture,' she agreed. 'I'd like to talk some more, but how long can a girl go on being the intended victim of a rape?'

She grinned knowingly, and extended the

automatic towards me. There was a loud crack, and I grabbed at myself, only to realize there was no pain. I heard a cry of anguish, and there was Cornelia, bleeding at the shoulder, and using language I hadn't heard since Korea.

In the doorway, Aunt Emma sat, hunched over an ancient Winchester repeater, crying.

'Young man,' she wept, 'you'll be getting a real bad impression of this family.'

*   *   *

Hours later, when the sheriff and his crew had disappeared, along with Cornelia, Aunt Emma said:

'It's hardly worth going to bed, is it?'

I looked at my watch. It wanted ten minutes of five in the morning.

'Aunt Emma,' I croaked, 'I'm not a dramatic person, but frankly I've had about all I can take for now. If you won't be offended, I'll just stretch out on this sofa for an hour or two.'

She didn't answer me directly. Instead, she muttered, half to herself,

'You know, I've been trying to recall what happened after Anthea ran off with that sharpie. Or rather,' she corrected, 'after I was told she'd run off. Cornelia said we had to get our minds off it. Had to concentrate, she said, on something completely new. So we started building the rockery.'

I nodded sympathetically. The old lady had had enough. That was obvious. I, too, had had enough. To me, that was even more obvious.

'Sure,' I intoned, 'rockery. That must have been it.'

Aunt Emma fixed me with one of her stares, and even at five a.m. that is quite an experience.

'Do you have any idea how many rockeries there are hereabouts? No, you do not. Let me tell you, they are rare. In fact, I am quite proud of mine. Not that you would understand that either.'

She was quite right, I didn't. But I didn't care either, at that moment.

'It never struck me at the time,' she bored on, 'Cornelia was never one for gardening. But now, as I think back, it suddenly takes on a new significance. Are you listening?'

I was stretched out on the sofa.

'Sure. I'm listening,' I mumbled. 'Tomorrow, in the morning, we're going to make a rockery.'

CHAPTER SIXTEEN

I stood in the shade on the verandah, watching the men work. There were four of them, stripped to the waist, bodies glistening in the sun as they swung their shovels rhythmically.

To one side, the sheriff leaned against a patrol car, chewing on a soggy cigar butt. The car radio crackled briefly, and the sheriff leaned inside to take the call.

'You realize I may be wrong about this.'

I turned to find that Aunt Emma was wheeling her chair towards me. I moved to help her but she waved me away.

'Don't fuss, young man. People fuss around me far too much. I'm an old woman, and I'm going to die. But I'm not going to sit around twiddling my thumbs waiting for it to happen. Do you think they'll find anything?'

'I don't know, ma'am,' I admitted. 'Seems a fairly long shot to me.'

'I know. But I remember after Anthea ran off with that awful man, I was so upset I didn't know what to do. It was Cornelia's idea we should occupy our minds. And our hands. Started it herself, heaving great lumps of rock from all over the place. After a while, I began to help. All these years I've tended it, looked after it myself till I became too ill. Then I always had a man do it. Looked nice, too.'

She said the last wistfully, watching one of the men straining at a large piece of rock. It came away suddenly, tearing out with it a whole batch of the clinging pink plants.

I looked at her face, wondering what it was costing her inwardly to watch the work of years being torn apart. And perhaps for nothing.

'Now don't you come out in this heat

upsetting yourself Miss Emma. You go on back in the house, and I'll be sure to come and let you know the minute we find—that is, the minute there's anything to tell you.'

The sheriff had come over, and was leaning on the wooden rail. Aunt Emma swung her head towards him.

'Now, see here Tom Fenwick. Don't you dare come around here sassing me in my own house. Just because some halfwit gave you a badge don't give you no right to tell me what to do. I chased you away a hundred times for stealing my apples. I can do it again if I have to.'

The sheriff grinned good-humoredly, looked quickly at me to see if I was laughing at him. He needn't have worried. I don't laugh at sheriffs very much.

'Danged if I don't believe you would too. Oh, Mr. Preston, you got a minute?'

'Sure.'

We walked a few yards away, out into the sun. I envied the sheriff his broad hat. He accepted an Old Favorite, throwing away the chewed cigar. Striking a match on his pants, he held out the flame.

'This is a queer business,' he muttered, 'I don't like it. Don't seem hardly right digging around Miss Emma's place for corpses.'

'I agree,' I told him. 'But it was all her own idea, you know. I tried to talk her out of it. She said no, if her niece was supposed to be dead she wanted it proved. Don't know whether I hope you find her or not.'

'What do you mean by that?'

He was treating the cigaret just like the stogie, rolling it wetly from one side of his mouth to the other.

'It'll be a shock to the old lady if you do find her,' I explained. 'On the other hand she'll never rest easy if you don't.'

'Know what you mean. Whichever side it flips, she loses. Shame. A tough old lady, but good. You know?'

'I know.'

'Tell me, all that stuff you said in your statement last night, is that all on the level? I mean, not doubting your word and all that, but that's a hell of a statement.'

It would be, I reasoned, to a country sheriff who probably broke up two bar fights every Saturday night, and that was what passed for a crime wave.

'It's a hell of a statement,' I conceded. 'But then, she's a hell of a woman, that one. I've seen 'em before, but not often. When you get a woman who's real bad, that's quite something. Anyway, you'll be getting confirmation from other forces. Monkton and Vale will both be able to bear out certain parts of it.'

'I know,' he returned ruefully. 'I've had them both on the 'phone already, claiming she belongs to them. This ought to stir up quite some dust around here. Trouble is, I ain't absolutely sure which one has the prior claim. Have to see the mayor about it.'

'Of course, you know your own business best,' I told him. 'But if you find that body, there's no question of priorities. She's all yours.'

His face took on a startled look.

'Say, that's right ain't it? I mean, this here murder, if there is any murder, why that was years before anything else. Say.'

His eyes looked far away, and I could guess what he was thinking. Big murder trial, right there in Little Falls. Newspaper men, television people, lawyers from the other cities. Picture in all the papers, maybe on the little square box. 'Sheriff Tom Fenwick, the arresting officer.'

'Could be quite a big event hereabouts, I imagine.'

'Yeah,' he breathed. 'That it could. Now come on, you men, we don't want to spend all day here.'

He strode across to the toilers, unconsciously straightening his back as he went. Man wants to look his best if he's going to appear on television. The old lady watched from the shade.

I went and stood near her, but she didn't seem to want to talk.

'Tom, hey Tom.'

One of the diggers looked up and beckoned the sheriff. Fenwick walked up to him, and

236

they both stood looking down. I threw away my cigaret, and went over to where they were standing. The other men joined us. Sticking out from the side of the hole was the skeleton of a hand.

'Looks like a hand,' muttered Fenwick. 'All right now, the rest of you. Spread yourselves along either side here, and start digging. Not rough now, take it nice and easy. If there's anything in here we want it all in one piece.'

The soil was very sandy, and came away easily as the men scraped and poked at it. Ten minutes later both feet were uncovered, and the other arm. There was only the foot or so of soil on top of the main body to remove. Nobody spoke now, there were no more jokes, no whistling.

'Jees.'

One of them stopped and swore quickly. We all looked at the red shiny material which he'd found.

'Looks like part of a raincoat,' whispered another.

'Tom, I'm sorry,' said the man, 'I'm, I'm—'

He turned and walked quickly away. Nobody jeered.

Fenwick's face was white now under the tan.

'All right boys, let's keep calm,' he muttered. 'We none of us like this, but it has to be done. Quick now, let's get it finished.'

Reluctantly, they carried on. It was a raincoat, hanging loosely around the skeleton.

The head was last, and this brought a low buzz from everyone, because the gold-colored hair was intact.

'I guess it's her, huh Tom?'

Fenwick recovered himself and snapped:

'Her? Of course it's her. How many corpses you think we have around here? All right men, that's it. Thanks for helping, you're through here now.'

Straightening up, he looked at me.

'Miss Emma'll have to know,' he said pointedly.

'You want me to tell her?'

'Well, er . . .' he hesitated, 'I ought to dig around a little more, see if there's anything else here.'

I walked back to the house, to where the old lady sat.

'It's her, isn't it? You've found her.'

'We think so,' I told her gently. 'Did she have a red raincoat?'

'I want to see her,' she replied.

'I really don't see what good it would do—' I protested.

'You'll have to carry me. Ground's too soft for this thing.'

I picked her up carefully, a frail old lady who only seemed to weigh a few pounds. Gently I walked over to where a few bones were wrapped up in red cloth. Aunt Emma stared down, unblinking. Then she nodded.

'It's her. That's her coat, and I couldn't

238

mistake the hair. The poor little thing. Poor, poor little thing.'

Her voice caught, and I thought she was going to cry. Instead, she shook her head impatiently.

'Better take me back, young man. I must be getting heavy.'

As I put her down in the wheelchair again, a solitary tear welled up and rolled unheeded down the lined old face. Sheriff Fenwick had been busy at his car radio. Now he waved me over to join him.

'Doc's on his way out here,' he told me importantly. 'First thing is to get a death certificate.'

I did a double take, to be sure he wasn't pulling my leg, but his face remained impassive.

'Who'll look after Aunt Emma now?' I asked.

'There's a nurse coming out this afternoon. She'd have been here earlier, only she's finishing up another case first.'

I looked back at the shaded verandah, where I knew the old lady was watching. One million dollars, I reflected, and the only person to look after you had to be a paid nurse.

'Well sheriff, if you don't have any more need for me around here, I ought to be heading home.'

'Sure thing. Mind, you'll be needed at the trial. Important witness, you're gonna be. You wouldn't be about to go on vacation to Japan or anything?'

The momentary panic in his voice made me smile inwardly. The idea of his important witness being missing when his big moment came was evidently of small appeal to Sheriff Fenwick.

'Not me,' I assured him. 'I'll be around when you want me.'

He stuck out a beefy fist, and shook hands enthusiastically.

'Been a real pleasure, Mr. Preston. I mean it. Be seeing ya—'

I nodded and went over to Aunt Emma.

'Well, Aunt Emma, I ought to be on my way.'

'Yes, of course. Have a safe journey.'

Turning to go, I swung round again.

'Er, I was wondering, er, if ever I'm round this way again, maybe I could kind of drop in and say hallo.'

She didn't answer immediately, but sat there staring at the dusty ground. When she spoke, her voice was small.

'I appreciate you mean that kindly, Mr. Preston. Yes, I appreciate that. And I know in this world a man has to do what he has to do. Yesterday, I didn't know you. I'd never even laid eyes on you. Yesterday, I had two nieces. One with me, one out somewhere in the world. Then you came, and now both my nieces are gone. I'm not saying that's any fault of yours.

240

Badness is badness. But I'm an old woman, and I haven't long to go. It would have been nice if—if—' She stopped and waited. 'No, Mr. Preston, I don't believe I want to see you again.'

Understanding, I nodded. Then I walked to the Chev and climbed in. The inside was like a furnace. As I rolled past the patrol car, the sheriff waved an arm.

Hours of hard driving away would be Louise. There'd be the cool sea, sand to lay around on, cold drinks. Later, maybe some music and other things. It was all a very long way from Orange Patch, helpless old ladies and corpses stretched out in the sun. What was it Aunt Emma had said? A man has to do what he has to do.

I gunned the motor as I reached the main highway. Yeah. But he doesn't always have to like it.